Kristina J.A. von Hofsten

Lena

Or, the Stark family. A sketch of real life.

Kristina J.A. von Hofsten

Lena
Or, the Stark family. A sketch of real life.

ISBN/EAN: 9783337331467

Printed in Europe, USA, Canada, Australia, Japan

Cover: Foto ©Andreas Hilbeck / pixelio.de

More available books at **www.hansebooks.com**

LENA:

OR,

THE STARK FAMILY.

A Sketch of Real Life.

FROM THE SWEDISH OF H. HOFSTEN.

BY

CARL LARSEN.

CINCINNATI:
HITCHCOCK AND WALDEN.
NEW YORK: NELSON & PHILLIPS.
1876.

EDITOR'S PREFACE.

IN human society, education is not limited to the school-room. We take our bias from our circumstances, from the people with whom we mingle, and from the opinions of our parents and elders. We have two opposite lines of conduct marked out for us; the one by the Church, the other by the world. The one promises us position, power, influence over others, wealth and pleasure; the other demands humility, self-denial, service and toil; but the end of the one is death and of the other, life.

In the following pages are pointed out these two ways and the classes of people pursuing them; the influences which educate for the world and the agencies that educate for Christ; the unsatisfactory portion of those who make knowledge, fashion and fame their highest good, and the repose and quiet of those who have given themselves to God and live in him. No sermon is so effective as a good example. God's children are God's witnesses; and a pure, holy, and loving life is more than miracles, than the gift of prophecy, than the knowledge of all mysteries. It was not by subtle argument that Axel was won to the faith. "Science falsely so called" drove him from it; a Christian life recovered him to it. And herein is the moral of the whole story: "Not by might nor by power, but by my Spirit, saith the Lord."

CONTENTS.

PAGE.

CHAPTER I.

United, yet Separated—Separated, yet United, . 9

CHAPTER II.

What occurs Gradually occurs Quietly, . . 22

CHAPTER III.

God moves in a Mysterious Way, ... 34

CHAPTER IV.

The Dawn of a New Day, ... 46

CHAPTER V.

Summer in the Country, ... 53

CHAPTER VI.

The Tutor, ... 63

CHAPTER VII.

LEARNED, AND YET IGNORANT, ... 78

PAGE.

CHAPTER VIII.

POISON OF UNBELIEF, ... 86

CHAPTER IX.

HONEY UPON THE LIPS, WORMWOOD IN THE HEART, . 96

CHAPTER X.

THE JOURNEY TO MARSTRAND, ... 107

CHAPTER XI.

"MY LIFE IS A WAVE," 121

CHAPTER XII.

TRUTH AND FALSEHOOD, ... 135

CHAPTER XIII.

THE MEETING, ... 146

CHAPTER XIV.

"BE NOT WISE IN THINE OWN EYES," . . . 159

CHAPTER XV.

VANITY, ... 171

CONTENTS.

CHAPTER XVI.

PAGE.

A Maternal Heart, ... 179

CHAPTER XVII.

Designs and Deliberations, ... 192

CHAPTER XVIII.

"Boast not of the Day before the Evening," . 199

CHAPTER XIX.

Taking Leave, ... 211

CHAPTER XX.

Homeward Bound, ... 221

CHAPTER XXI.

"All is Well that ends Well," 225

ILLUSTRATIONS.

PAGE.

AUNT LENA AND ELSIE, ... *Frontispiece.*

AUNT LENA AND HER MOTHER, ... 44

AFTER THE BALL, ... 119

ELSIE AND MRS. BILLMER, ... 215

LENA:

OR,

THE STARK FAMILY.

Chapter I.

UNITED, YET SEPARATED—SEPARATED, YET UNITED.

IGHT years had passed since Clara Stark entered, as a bride, her wealthy but cheerless home. Soon forever she must leave it. Yes, soon! she felt this. She had often heard "the falling of leaves" spoken of in connection with the death of other consumptives; and to her question, whether this time were fraught with peculiar danger to herself, she received from the physician a grave reply that confirmed her apprehensions.

From her window she could see but little of the sky; yet, above roofs and chimneys, she

perceived heavy October clouds, and the dark,
dirty street gave equal evidence of the presence
of Autumn. The prospect was so dull and
damp that she shuddered involuntarily, and,
drawing her shawl more tightly around her,
took her accustomed place upon the sofa, where
now was spent the greater portion of the day.

With half-closed eyes, she relapsed into retro-
spection. She thought of the happiness of her
childhood in the unpretending paternal home
away there—far away, it seemed to her—near
by the fresh, rustling woods; where, a child,
she had played with the pine-cones, plucked
strawberries and flowers, and sat long whiles
listening to the whisperings of nature. That
these were about God, she knew full well, but
was unable to comprehend the language.

Often, at a later day, a similar feeling overcame her while perusing her Bible. There was
the rustling of a powerful spirit; words from
God, and about God. As a little child again,
she sat listening, feeling herself an infinitesimal,
yet at the same time infinitely safe. Her theo-
retical knowledge of spiritual things was small;
but this she knew: that the Savior of the world
had lived, suffered, and died for her; and her
conviction concerning this was so firm as to
enable her, without a shudder, to view the ap-

proach of death. How she had attained to such a degree of faith she hardly knew; for without human guidance had been her search for light and truth. Christian communion, with its blessings and temptations, was no part of her experience. Thought of death had been the preacher that aroused her, and God's own Word her teacher and comforter. Her sensitive spirit had, ere finding peace, encountered few struggles; so few that, had she opened her heart to some older Christian, who had met severe struggles, he would perhaps have warned her, and endeavored to show that a peace so easily acquired must be a false one. But from such a trial she was spared, and with child-like confidence clung to Him who has declared that the smoking flax he will not quench, nor break the bruised reed.

From the sunny scenes of childhood, her thoughts moved forward. The fresh, poetic wood gave place to other pictures; she saw herself, a tender, withering plant, in a renowned boarding-school. Studies, reprimands, school-girl intrigues, stolen opportunities for fictitious reading, and bad fare, were the recollections of this period, from which she turned with indifference.

Again stepped forth her early home, as it

was when her age was sixteen, and her education
looked upon as completed. How her heart
throbbed with joy when, at her return from
school, the old familiar gate opened on its grat-
ing hinges, welcoming her to Paradise—so it
seemed! How happy was she in the embrace
of her parents, and were all, at her return—
old Stina, who stood in the kitchen doorway,
wiping away her tears with her apron; Lawrence—the homely, honest Lawrence—who, in
ecstasy at again beholding Miss Clara, laughed
so heartily that his eyes seemed to retire modestly, in making way for the broad smile; and
Tusse, the watch-dog, whose demonstrations
were so violent as to cause a big hole in her
dress, and almost tumble her over! And what
pies she got! O, all was so rich and nice!

A faint smile illuminated the features of the
sufferer at these reminiscences; but the pictures
soon became obscured. The joy of the return
was succeeded by a certain sense of void. She
had neither brother nor sister, nor regular occupation. She needed "repose"—so her parents
thought—and the repose she took was abandon-
ment to dreams and fiction.

To be sure, when seated with her book in
the wood, the rustling in the fir-trees above her
head was as solemn as of yore; but she listened

not as then. Her imagination was ever filled with variegated pictures; and the monotonous life at home, the quiet, great life in nature, seemed to her colorless and empty. Many a time had she dropped her book and sighed at her misfortune—the possession of a good, quiet home. How uninteresting and insignificant her existence seemed! But, amid her idle dreaming, grief suddenly came. Her father died. The little property was sold, and she removed, with her mother, to Stockholm, there to live upon the interest of the little capital left them by the father.

Well, she had got so far as to be poor and unhappy. However, this was much less romantically interesting than she had imagined. The small rooms, the daily cares in making the money reach, the missing of the father, the constant complaints of the mother,—all this was far more dispiriting than the quiet life at Skogsvig.

One day she was sitting alone, thinking, as ever, upon her heroines, wondering if any of them had led such a tiresome life as was hers, when there came a knock at the door. She opened it, and saw before her a gentleman, with light, smoothly combed hair, and large spectacles, through which looked forth a pair of earnest, pale-blue eyes.

How tiresome she thought he appeared! How well she remembered the oppressive silence that followed the self-introduction as merchant Stark, and invitation to be seated, for "mother would be in immediately;" and, finally, when mother appeared, the chitchat concerning matters which she did not understand. How her mother thanked him, with tears, "that he would be a protector to two poor, defenseless ones;" and how reluctant he seemed at the knightly character her mother would attribute to him, assuring her that her affairs were in such an orderly condition, and so easily managed, he could see nothing to protect them from!

And so he took leave, but often returned. Sometimes she wondered, "Why?" He had so little to say! But one day he came, looking, if possible, more smoothly brushed than usual, and asked for her hand. Her mother consented, with undisguised pleasure, while herself sat as if paralyzed by lightning.

She felt her hand placed in his, her mother's embrace, and heard her benediction; felt his arm placed awkwardly and timidly around her waist, his kiss upon her forehead. And so she was engaged. To be sure, she afterward aroused from her passive compliance, and told her mother it was impossible that she should become the wife of the merchant; but the mother's tears and entreaties prevailed. And, after all, there was something pleasing to her overwrought fancy in the thought that she was sacrificing herself for her mother, and becoming so deeply, so touchingly unhappy.

With a sting of conscience, she remembered how joy had beamed from the merchant's earnest eyes during the brief period of their engagement, and when, as a husband, he conducted her to his home, her feeling of captivity as she saw the large, dark rooms, with the rich, heavy curtains, admitting so sparingly the dim October light, the massive furniture, the pent-up air; how he turned to her, to find some look of appreciative pleasure, and she burst into tears.

Thus began their married life; and had its continuance been like its commencement? Alas! yes. She felt as depressed and strange in her husband's presence now as then, and the expression of joy had never returned to his eye as it rested upon her. Upon his children he could look with pleasure and love. If he had only been wont to bestow upon her the same fervent look as upon them, then —

Here her meditations were interrupted by the clatter of little feet, and a fine, healthy-looking boy of six years came running toward her.

"Mamma," he cried, "we have been out to walk—O, so far off—and you can't think how nice it was! The trees are so handsome, and have so many colors, and the falling leaves go dancing and whirling as if they were alive. And I've seen so many apples; and I bought four with my own money. I wanted to stay longer; but Kirsten said it was going to rain, and it was 'most dinner-time, and that you were so lonely, sweet mamma."

Kirsten, the nurse, and, moreover, a pretty important personage in the house, now entered, with the baby, Elsie, who extended her fat arms toward her mother.

Could Clara have seen the beaming, lovely expression of her own countenance, as she looked upon her children, the thought would perhaps have occurred, "Have I ever looked thus at my husband?" and her conscience would have replied, "No, no!"

"Do you know, mamma, Elsie can almost walk alone? See, mamma!" said Axel, and opened his arms to receive the little one, who really, with some tottering steps, came into his embrace, winding her arms around his neck.

"See, see, mother!" cried Axel. "She came so willingly to me, although I hadn't any thing to coax her with. Kirsten holds out candy and toys to her; but she likes me best."

The mother smiled, while tears filled her eyes.

"My own boy," said she, "may you ever remain thus loving toward your sister! Soon I must leave my little children so lonely in the world. God's love watches over you; but don't forget to love—love—"

She was interrupted by a violent cough. The tired head sank back upon the pillow, and a stream of blood issued from her pale lips.

With an exclamation of dread, Axel pressed his sister so tightly in his arms that she began to cry. The excited old nurse hurriedly lifted the babe in her arms, and, giving Axel a push, to accelerate his exit, cried:

"Out of the room—do you hear? There is misery enough here, without you getting up a scene, and frightening the poor baby."

The children were left alone, in the dark, uncomfortable nursery. Elsie soon cried herself asleep; but Axel sat there, pale and still, with his large, dark eyes fixed upon the door, and his little hands clinched while he listened. First, he heard quick steps through doors and stairways; then the squeaking of his father's boots, in a manner that denoted great hurry, and the

sound of each step fell upon his ears like a
short, sharp cry.   A while after, a carriage
stopped outside.   He recognized the steps of
the doctor, who also was in a hurry.

It began to grow dark.   The expected rain
fell in heavy drops, rolling adown the window-
panes like big tears.   All seemed so anxious
and cold.

"Soon I must leave my little children lonely
in the world," mother had said.   The words
resounded in Axel's memory, and he felt them
so bitter and heavy.   "Had she perhaps already
gone away?"   He must see her.   He sprang
up, opened the door, and went quickly through
the dark passage.   Outside the sick-room he
paused.   His heart throbbed.   His little frame
quivered.   Should he venture?   Yes; the door
slowly opened.   No one saw him.   He glided
forward into the shade of the bed-curtains, and
found his father and mother alone in the dimly
lighted room.   He could see, through the open
door, the doctor and Kirsten, standing in the
anteroom, silent and grave, before the stove, in
which the fire was merrily blazing, seeming in
such contrast with the surrounding gloom.

Axel heard his father's voice, broken by sobs,
and so mild he could hardly recognize it.

"Clara, can you forgive me?   I have made

your life so unhappy. You have been very dear to me, but I have never had the courage and ability to make it manifest to you. You can never comprehend what I have suffered from my own awkward reserve. Your poor mother not only herself imagined that you were fortunate, but caused me to do the same. And you, poor little child! you, alas, sacrificed yourself, without opening your mouth in one cry of anguish. Why were not my eyes opened before it was too late? You have never complained; but think you not that I have seen how your youth has faded and dissolved in tears? Clara, can you forgive?"

"Hush, hush! you must n't speak so. I have nothing to forgive," whispered the sick one. "I see every thing now so clearly. I have been unhappy because I have been boundlessly selfish. I have reveled in pain, without a thought that my husband, too, could suffer. It is I who have made you unhappy. Thank God, he has shown me the enormity of my sin at the same time with forgiveness. Yes; grace I experience, only the grace of God's merciful love. He has forgiven me, and will you?"

A smile of hope lighted the pallid countenance. The feeble arms were extended, and in a long embrace they were clasped who so long had been united, and yet had been separated.

But the exertion proved too great. The peaceful, solemn silence was interrupted by a violent cough. Again there was anxiety and stir in the sick-room, and the little pale listener was discovered, but not to be punished or pushed away. It was the father who perceived him, took his little hand within his own, and said, tenderly:

"Come, my little boy, let us sit here. We can't help mamma; but we can look at her, if only we don't get in the doctor's way."

Axel felt so honored and proud at this familiar "we," that, in his childish inability to comprehend grief, he sat upon the sofa quite contented, considering, with the eye of a general, all that transpired in the room.

Soon all was still again. The sick one fell into a deep slumber. The others sat, silently waiting. The old clock, with its rattling sound, seemed rapidly measuring off the last hours of the young woman's life. Yet a few more, and the inquietude of time to her would have ceased.

Death approached, solemnly, secretly; not as a messenger of judgment, but as one from Him who has said, "I am the resurrection and the life;" and, before the moment of departure, Axel was wrapped in the healthful, quiet slumber of childhood.

Chapter II.

WHAT OCCURS GRADUALLY, OCCURS QUIETLY.

THE day succeeding his wife's death, merchant Stark wrote to his only sister, Miss Lena, asking her to come and undertake the superintendence of his household. While his wife was yet living, he had proffered her a home with him; but his invitation had been firmly declined. She believed herself more useful where she was, and feared that the society of an elderly sister-in-law might seem uncongenial to his young wife. Now that she was needed, she was immediately ready to come.

But, before her entrance to her brother's family, it may be well to make her acquaintance. Unaffected, upright, and industrious, she had struggled through life. The roses of youth had long before disappeared from her cheeks, if, indeed, they had ever bloomed there. One felt tempted to believe, rather, that her *entrée* to the

world had been made with the same weather-
beaten exterior that now characterized her, and
reminded one of storms and rough weather.
Not as if herself were the "storm-awakening
power." No; she was quiet ever, like her
brother; but one could see that her life had
comprised not many sunny days; yet, notwithstanding, her eye contained a look of cheerfulness which inspired confidence; and knowledge
of direction was perceptibly a leading feature of
her life.

Her childhood was spent in a home of poverty and care. Her father was a person of weak
character, who drank and wept, was intoxicated
and sentimental, during the whole day. Her
mother, on the contrary, was energetic, des-
potic, and violent, hesitating not, in presence
of her children, to express to her husband her
contempt for his weakness.

Lena, the eldest child, the only sister of two
brothers, became early familiar with self-denial
and toil. With the never-to-be-restricted sense
of justice possessed by a child, she could but
pity and despise her father, while she blamed
the conduct, yet respected the energy, of her
mother.

Thus many years passed away. The quiet,
industrious girl grew to the age of sixteen. Her

father had gone to a drunkard's grave. His death was one of those horrible scenes, so oft repeated, yet ineffectual to turn from their course those who tread the path of vice. Lena sat, trembling, beside the sick-bed, listening to her father's horrible fancies, and saw, with dread, death's solemn silence interrupt the restless struggle.

She pondered upon his fate, and upon her own. Then, one day, her eye fell upon the old, dusty Bible; and she determined to seek there an answer to the many questions that disturbed her thoughts. Her first effort was very discouraging. She read and sought; but what she found was neither light nor peace. She was impressed with a sense of the holiness and justice of God, while her own condition seemed increasingly wretched. However, continuity was a part of her character, and she kept on. In the poor home, there was little time for reading; yet no day passed without her having given a little to the perusal of her Bible.

One Sunday forenoon, she sat alone at home. The scantily furnished little room was clean and peaceful, and the sun shone brightly upon the flowers in the window; but Lena's heart seemed heavier than usual. Her mother had censured her for "hanging over the Bible;"

her younger brother had annoyed her with his merriment; the elder one (the merchant) had, the day previous, left home to begin to earn his bread. Through the assistance of relatives, he had obtained a situation in Stockholm, and was, consequently, far away from his little native town, lying there, in a forgotten corner, never dreaming of its future greatness, when railroad and telegraph should put it in connection with the rest of the world. To Lena, all now seemed empty; for Gustav was the only one who had understood her.

The Bible lay open before her. She read; but her thoughts were not there, and the act seemed like a work of thralldom, without life or hope. Her perseverance tottered. A sense of being alone, sinful and lost, overcame her. After turning the leaves backward and forth for a while, she pushed the book from her, forever she thought, and, with this act, the last plank of safety. In despairing anguish, her head sank upon the table, and tears deluged her pale cheeks, when, suddenly, from the depths of her heart, arose a prayer, dim and groping, but full of life: "Lord, have mercy! Lord, help!" and she was brought to experience the truth of the promise, "While yet they call, I will answer." He who calmed the tempest of Gen-

nesaret, calmed also the tempest of her heart;
and, in blessed wonder, she felt that for her,
too, there was grace, pardon, and peace. She
raised her head, and her eye fell upon the open
Bible, which, so shortly before, she had pushed
from her; and, drawing it to her, she read:
"Fear not: for I have redeemed thee. I have
called thee by thy name; thou art mine." These
words were so plain an assurance of the presence of God's Spirit, speaking in her heart, that
it seemed as if she more heard than read them.

She was sitting thus, when her mother returned from Church, and, with an unkind push,
exclaimed:

"Are you asleep, this bright Sunday morning, when other decent people are in church!
You ought to have heard how the minister
spoke about our duties, and the pleasure of
dying, when one can look back upon a life well
spent, and think of all the good he has done.
That is preaching one can understand and appre-
ciate. Yes, it was something different from that
of the ranter whom the Lundgrens fooled me to
go and hear, last week. He cried at people, how
wicked they were, and almost got me to believe
I was no better than a robber or a murderer.
What are you gazing at? You stare at me, as if
you didn't understand me! Aren't you awake?"

"Yes, I am awake for the first time in my life; and, with God's help, I shall not sleep again," replied Lena, rising to go out into the kitchen and resume the forgotten preparation for dinner.

Now it was the mother's turn to stare at Lena. She would have liked to relieve herself of a multitude of words; but the daughter's countenance had bespoken such holy earnestness, that the mother, contrary to habit, felt compelled to silence.

This Sunday was the turning-point in Lena's life. The light that then beamed in her soul was never extinguished. To be sure, it shone not always equally bright. Many clouds of discouragement in her heart, as in the hearts of other Christians, would arise, hiding the sun of grace; but night never again prevailed there. Gladly would she have persuaded her parent to be a partaker of the blessedness she had found; but the mother's high opinion of her own sufficiency was a barrier which the gentle, unassuming daughter could not demolish.

Lena went quietly forward, hoping that God would use other means for the performance of a work to which she was unequal, when only, in firm trust, she invoked his aid. Thus she waited long, without wearying in prayer. Year after year rolled away, and the answer to the petition came; but the messengers that brought it were not smiling angels. Their names were sickness, grief, pain, want, and death.

The strong, self-reliant Mrs. Stark was laid upon a bed of illness, weak and helpless as a child. At first, she resolved to bear the misfortune well, as she believed she had her other vicissitudes; but the difficulties increased, and her helplessness accordingly. Her mind became filled with bitterness and complaint. The family expenses grew, and, consequent upon her illness, the income diminished; for, although from Gustav came small contributions of money, their main dependence was the combined earnings of the mother and daughter. Now, while the former lay ill, much of the time of the latter was occupied in nursing her.

But one sunbeam remained — happy, kind Fritz, not only the pet of mother and sister, but, one could almost say, of the whole place. With honor he had gone through the preparatory school course, and was ready for Upsala University in the Fall; but, at present, he was acting as tutor in the family of Judge ——, where he was a great favorite. The village druggist, a rich old bachelor, who was his godfather, had hinted at a design to leave him the greater part of his property, and promised to bear the expenses of his collegiate course; for his plan was to study medicine. Many a time was the gloom that prevailed in his mother's sick-room dispelled by his cheerfulness.

One day, as was his habit, he came running up the rickety stairs that led to his mother's room, and always, with a peculiar squeak, announced to the expectant ones his coming.

"Welcome, my boy!" cried his mother. "How late you are to-day; but the weather is so fine, no wonder, that, in the open air, the young forget those, who, lying upon the couch of pain, can get no more of the Summer than flies, and the effluvia of the gutter, whenever the window is opened."

"O, little ma," replied Fritz, "you are really unjust. I was late, to-day, just because I remembered you. See what a bouquet I have brought you! I wish I had its duplicate for my bride on my wedding-day; and each individual rose I plucked from Judge ——'s garden, that you may have a little taste of the Summer, dear mother."

"Thank you, Fritz," said Lena. "See how beautiful it looks, upon the table, beside mamma's bed."

"I have suffered more pain than usual," said

the mother. "I have been alone nearly the whole forenoon. Lena has been out in the kitchen, baking; but I believe she has been hanging over some book, or she could have looked in upon me a little oftener."

Lena took her sewing, without making reply, while Fritz, distressed for his sister, hastened to turn conversation in another direction.

"What a pity I have n't finished my studies," said he, "so I could rid mamma of her pains, and procure myself world-wide renown. Would n't that be nice, mamma? I 've been tempted to give up medicine. I believe I would rather be a minister; I could do more good."

"I have always thought," said Lena, "that no one had better opportunity for doing good than a doctor."

"That is so," said Fritz. "I was not in earnest; I would n't relinquish my chosen vocation. May I only be able rightly to fill it!"

As he spoke, his youthful countenance wore a look of such earnestness and hope as to cause from Lena's heart a glad thanksgiving to rise. She seemed to perceive in the young man's soul the dawn of a new life. Upon the mother, his earnestness produced a quite different impression. It awoke a vague fear. What was the matter with her happy boy? Had some one been putting extravagant scruples into his head?

Fritz turned to Lena, and suddenly interrupted the silence:

"Did you go to the Bible-class, last evening?" he asked.

"No," replied Lena, with a little sigh.

"No!" exclaimed the mother; "I will not have it. Lena has more liberty than most girls of her age"—in what the liberty consisted, was an enigma—"but such carryings-on as the new vicar has introduced, I can not but utterly disapprove. To go, in the middle of the week, to church, instead of attending to one's business, is certainly a misuse of time."

A mischievous smile shone from the eye of Fritz, as he replied:

"For my part, I must confess that I really neglected something, by sitting in church from seven to eight, last evening. Can you forgive me, mamma, for forgetting an invitation?"

"Would you have taken part in such an affair as that last night?"

"Why not?" replied Fritz. "But, you see, in the afternoon, a lady friend asked me to accompany her, in the evening, to church; and I could n't refuse. I thought there would be plenty of time for the entertainment afterward;

and, if I had had any desire for it, I suppose
there would have been; but I was so impressed
by what I heard at church, I forgot all about it.
The lesson was in first Corinthians, second chapter and first nine verses. You ought to have
heard the new vicar. He spoke of the enormity of sin, to have needed so great an atone-
ment. He took away all my pillars of morality;
but he did n't leave me there. He gave me a
firmer foundation to build upon. Then the con-
clusion! I wish I could tell you how he spoke
of what no eye hath seen and no ear heard,
that God has prepared for those who love him!"

Fritz became silent, and seemed absorbed in
thought upon what he had heard.

"Tell me, mamma," said he, after a while,
"did I do very wrong in neglecting the entertainment?"

"Have I said I wished you to go to a
carouse?" asked the mother. "You know that
I disapprove of them."

"Utterly, as of the Bible-class?" asked Fritz,
with a smile.

"Hush, saucy boy!" retorted the mother.
"It is in very bad taste to speak, at the same
time, upon things so opposite."

Mrs. Stark felt uneasy at the turn conversation
had taken, and knew that she had improperly

judged the Bible-class; but to acknowledge a mistake was a weakness of which she had never been guilty. Fritz perceived that a struggle was going on within his mother's mind; and, too tender to be willing to prolong it, he arose to go.

"Well," said he, "here I am sitting, forgetting my duties. It is after twelve o'clock; and I promised the little boys to take them out bathing to-day. I am teaching them to swim. They will soon be able to dive as well as I do; and you know I am like a fish, in the water. Good-bye! We shall meet again, soon."

For a moment was heard the sound of his quick step upon the street; and then stillness prevailed in the little chamber and out of doors— the drowsy stillness of the Summer noon. In the little room, the heat was oppressive. The flies buzzed. Lena's needle flew. She was happy at what she had heard from her brother; and earnestly she prayed that God would make him the means of blessing to her mother.

3

Chapter III.

GOD MOVES IN A MYSTERIOUS WAY.

S Mrs. Stark lay tossing upon her bed, her mind was racked with conflicting thoughts and emotions. Her son's words — but, yet more, his beaming look when he spoke of what he had heard and felt at church—had sunk into her heart; but should she rejoice or fear? Was it God working in him — God, for whom she felt a trembling awe—or was her happy boy to be a fanatic?

However, she had one reason for joy: he did not participate in the carouse, and, perhaps, would never acquire a taste for such scenes. Too well she remembered a youth with the same clear, blue eyes, the same merry laugh. He was the ideal of her youth, and became her husband. His vivacity, during the first years of their married life, was never shaded. But a little cloud appeared upon their horizon. The

34

happy husband sometimes came home to his young wife in unnatural glee; but he asked her pardon, and consoled her with the assurance that it was nothing remarkable when a young man of his temperament, in a merry company, drank a little more than was good for him. The cloud grew, the horizon of her life was darkly overcast, the storm burst upon them, and the once happy home was soon a sorrowful ruin. The long experience of poverty, humiliation, grief, bitterness, and misery, came up before her with frightful distinctness.

Had Fritz found a means for conquering the temptations that ruined his father?

Thus nearly an hour passed, when a hurried running upon the street gave to her thoughts a new direction.

"Who can that be, running so in the heat? Lena, go see what it means," said Mrs. Stark.

"It is Carlie Bogren; he has gone in to Dr. Dahl's."

"Well, you will see, then, that Mrs. Bogren has a fit. I have expected this a good while. I wonder who Mr. Bogren will get to take care of his large family. Has the doctor gone?"

"Yes; how he runs! but he has passed Mr. Bogren's house," replied Lena.

"Well, do n't sit there," said her mother; "find out where he is going."

The daughter removed her geranium from the window, and leaned out.

"They have passed the Judge's corner, and I can't see them more," said Lena, resuming her seat.

"Well," said the mother, "so Mrs. Bogren has n't got a fit yet; but what can it be? How wrong it is to frighten the sick by running so through the street! What if the Judge has had another attack? But I should think Fritz would let us know, if any thing is the matter there. Can't you throw on your bonnet, and run out a little way? You will be sure to meet somebody of whom you can ask."

"Let me just finish these last button-holes," said Lena; "then I can go with the shirts to the parsonage. I promised them to-day."

"O, well! I generally have to wait," said Mrs. Stark, impatiently; and, turning to the wall, she tried to sleep.

Lena continued at her sewing, but kept thinking of the little incident upon the street.

Finally, her work being finished, she arose to comply with her mother's wish, when, glancing from the window, she saw the Judge approaching. Her first impression was a feeling of pleasure that it was not he who had been taken ill; the next was surprise, on looking at him more closely. His countenance, naturally flushed and smiling, was very pale, and wore a look of anguish. His steps were slow and heavy, as if each one cost him an effort; and the nearer he came, the slower was his pace. He looked up to the window. Their eyes met. He stopped and beckoned; then covered his face with his hands, and burst into tears.

For a moment, Lena stood motionless with astonishment; at the next, she stood upon the street, beside the weeping man. She tried to speak; but her pale lips could only stammer,

"Fritz?"

"Yes, Miss Lena; God help me!" exclaimed the Judge. "I was to come and prepare you, but I am unfit; and so Miss Lena understands at once."

"What?" said Lena. "I understand nothing. Is Fritz sick?"

"No; he is dead."

"Dead!" Lena trembled violently; and she leaned against the porch.

"I am so inconsiderate! Forgive me," said the Judge. "I determined to speak very cautiously. He was drowned; or, no, he was not drowned, but perished while bathing. The doctor says he has had a blow upon the temple, that must have killed him instantly. There was an old anchor lying under water, and he has a bruise upon his temple. He was diving, and called upon my sons to mark the time of his absence under water. He was gone too long; and Carl, who knows how to dive, went in after him, but soon came up, bringing the lifeless body to the surface with him. The poor boy was so frightened he could hardly get into the boat. Alfred cried for help, and some laborers, who were taking their noon rest under a shade near by, heard him, sprang into a boat, and rowed out to the boys. By means of boat-hooks they drew up poor Fritz, and brought him home, where, for fear of giving us too great a shock, they laid him upon a seat in the arbor. Just as they were bringing him into the garden, Carlie Bogren came along, and they sent him for the doctor. My wife and I were sitting in the passage, wondering why the boys were so late to their dinner, when they came rushing in, pale and weeping. And when we were told what had happened, alas, Miss Lena! it was as if he had been my own—the dear, dear boy.! The doctor, who was on hand immediately, said that nothing could be done; but my wife went into a convulsion, and he had to remain with her, while I came here to prepare you, lest you should hear the dreadful tidings too suddenly. I meant to be very careful, yet told you so abruptly."

As he ceased speaking, big tears rolled down his cheeks, and the timid, retiring Lena threw her arms around his neck. A minute she gave free vent to her pain; but quickly her thoughts returned to her mother.

They entered together. Again the old stairway creaked, but not as when, a little while before, the joyous Fritz had trodden it.

The sick one, who through the open window had heard their voices, without being able to understand the words spoken, lay in anxious suspense, yet feeling a kind of satisfaction in exciting herself to anger at Lena for her slowness, and was ready to attack with upbraidings, as soon as the door should open. But the words died upon her lips as her eye fell upon the countenance of Lena, who seated herself beside the bed, and, taking her mother's hand between her own trembling ones, whispered:

"Mother, pray God for submission, and grace to enable you to bear the cross. His hand is upon us."

A deathly paleness overspread the mother's

countenance, and the sweat of anguish stood upon her forehead; but, in a voice clear and commanding, she exclaimed:

"Speak! tell all! You know I am strong."

"God has called Fritz to heaven," said Lena.

A wild shriek escaped the mother.

"It is not true; it can't be so," she cried. "My child! Where is my child?"

"He is with his Savior, mamma," replied Lena. "Do you remember how happy he was when he spoke about what no eye hath seen and no ear heard? Ought we not to thank God for so soon letting him go to his blessed home?"

"Thank? No, no; I can not thank! I can not bear this! it is too much, too much!" cried the mother.

"Try to say, God be merciful to me a sinner!" whispered Lena.

The mother became a little quiet—then exclaimed, suddenly and violently:

"You haven't told me how he died. He was here just a little while ago, healthy and happy."

Lena beckoned to the Judge, who stood in the doorway. He approached, and, tenderly taking the mother's hand, said:

"God strengthen you! His chastisement is

severe! but if he lays a burden upon us, he will also help us to bear it."

Then, seating himself beside her, he told her all, concluding by begging the mournful privilege of taking upon himself what must follow.

While he was speaking, the bereaved mother lay staring at him fixedly—deep, convulsive sighs being her only manifestation of life; but, as he concluded, she began to tremble violently, the hitherto tearless eyes filled with tears, and she wept—wept as one does when it seems as if the heart has swelled to bursting with its over-measure of pain.

Reader, hast thou ever thus experienced how an aching despair can, by some tender word from a warm, loving heart, be transformed to a grief that finds relief in tears?

The Judge now tenderly bade them adieu; and Lena sat upon a stool, reclining her head against the bed, absorbed in thought upon the blessedness of her brother, who, with contest so soon ended, could now exultingly exclaim:

"The snare is broken, and the bird set free!"

O, when should it be thus with her? Her imagination pictured a long, long way, darker and more difficult than ever; then, lifting her head and looking cheerfully forward, she saw that a few steps more or less mattered little, so

long as the goal was sure. She would not
murmur if God yet longer made use of her
upon earth. Was it not a privilege to be allowed to serve him who had borne her sins,
and whose love was her, blessed inheritance in
time and eternity?

She was wakened from her reveries by the
voice of her mother.

"Lena, Lena," said she, "you are right. I
need to cry, God be merciful to me a sinner!
He has crushed my proud self-righteousness.
I have boasted of my strength—I, frail, miserable creature of the dust. So he has laid
upon me this great affliction, which I can not
endure. No, Lord, I can not. Give me back
my child!"

And the violent look of despair returned.

"That is so, mamma," said Lena; "it is
impossible to carry the burden of both grief
and sin. But do n't you remember Jesus said,
'Come unto me, all ye who labor and are heavy
laden, and I will give you rest?'"

"Yes; but I can not come," said the mother.
"Alas! I am too much a stranger to him. It
is humiliating for me to acknowledge this to
you, whom I have so often silenced when you
wished to speak to me of him. I have told
you that I understood these things better than

you did. I was too proud to learn of you.
You knew this well enough; but what you did
not know was, how I suffered from envy of your
peace."

"Poor mamma," said Lena, "how unhappy
you have been! Why have you not fled to the
cross?"

"I have tried to pray," said the mother;
"but I fear my prayers have done me more
harm than good. I have either read prayers
that were only words to which my heart was a
stranger, or have spoken from it bitter words
of murmuring. It is no easy matter for me to
go to Christ."

"O mamma! He has already come to
you," said Lena. "See, he stands at the door
of your heart and knocks! Let us pray together."

And in simple, warm language, Lena prayed
for both, that their grief might be made to
them a blessing; and that they might come
to dwell together in the land of rest, where
the beloved son and brother had now preceded
them.

The mother whispered, "Amen!" and Lena
believed she saw the answer of her prayer
that God would make Fritz a means of blessing
to her mother; but how differently from what

she had expected did the answer come! She
had pictured for him a long, useful life, and
now she saw that through his death the blessing
was to be.

Lena hoped that now her mother would
better understand her, and that their life hence-
forward would be one of harmony; but "the
Old Adam" was, in Mrs. Stark, as tenacious
of life as in other of Adam's children. Her
natural disposition still became manifest, and,
although she struggled to subdue this enemy,
peace was often disturbed by it. But to Lena
a greater trial than this, to which she always
had been accustomed, was the difference that
now appeared in their religious tastes. The
quiet character of Lena's life, which spoke
not in words, but was stamped upon all her
actions, corresponded not with the mother's
restless desire for conversation; and the daughter was often upbraided for her inactivity and
silence, while she, on the contrary, wearied
of all the nonsensical prattle upon religious
subjects, introduced to the house by well-
meaning but simple-minded and talk-loving
friends.

Thus, in work and contest, passed many
years; but peace came at last. Both mother
and daughter were earnest Christians, and, as

Aunt Lena and her Mother.

their experience grew, they came nearer each other; so that, ere death terminated Mrs. Stark's many years of suffering, entire harmony prevailed in the little home.

Chapter IV.

THE DAWN OF A NEW DAY.

ALREADY has the reader's patience been too long taxed with the picture of a life so obscure as was that of Lena. We pass, therefore, the many years succeeding her mother's death, which were spent by her in assisting her friends in their various concerns of life. Now she made the bridal wreath, now mended the linen, hung the curtains, made the preserves, etc.; but most appreciated was Lena's presence by the sick-bed and in the house of mourning. Many, who in days of prosperity and health found the "good lady" somewhat tiresome and one-sided, stretched their arms longingly toward her in hours of pain and sorrow.

We now find her in the house of merchant Stark, to which her entrance was made a few days after the death of her sister-in-law; and with firm hand did she here seize the reins, to the great advantage and well-being of the house, although to the great dissatisfaction of the servants, who, during the previous weak management, had lived in unrestricted liberty. Even old Kirsten, who, in virtue of her quality as chamber-maid to the merchant in his bachelor days, and afterward nurse in his family, was accustomed to give free vent to her severity, had to resign to the quiet strength of Lena.

"Come, Axel," said the merchant, "this is Aunt Lena, who has come to take care of my little children in mother's place. Come and greet her."

Axel looked into Lena's face scrutinizingly, as he extended his tiny hand.

"But, papa," said he, "she is n't like mamma. I would rather go to my own mamma in heaven."

"My little friend," said Lena, with a smile that won the child's confidence, "that is just where we shall go together. Every day, we will knock at the door of heaven, and ask to be let in; but perhaps God will keep us waiting many years; and then we must n't be impatient, but good, obedient children, doing cheerfully all that he commands us."

"But how can we knock at the door of

heaven? It is so far up there," said Axel, looking inquiringly at Lena.

"With our prayers, dear," said Lena. "Jesus has promised that God will hear us; and you know that what he promises is always sure."

"Yes, mamma told me so," said Axel, confidingly.

Their conversation was interrupted, but had already laid, in Axel's heart, the foundation of a warm friendship for aunty, and a feeling of safety in her presence.

Soon after the funeral, the home of the Stark family assumed a different and brighter aspect. All vestige of sickness was removed; each nook and corner dusted, aired, and arranged. The uncomfortable nursery was abandoned; and the large chamber, that, with its heavy bed-curtains, had seemed so dark, was transformed to a nursery, where merry plays took the place of the sighs and tears that before had so often sought concealment in its solitude.

Was, then, the young wife and mother already forgotten? No. One corner there was inaccessible to the sun of heaven and brushes of earth. It was the heart of the husband. The merchant, more than formerly, gave himself to the society of his children. His sorrow was too deep for the cold atmosphere of business life. His soul needed warmth; and, as the word of the highest love was to him a dark saying, he sought it in the reflection of the divine that met him in the souls of his children. Hour after hour would he sit watching them, and listening to Axel's merry prattle; and sometimes there came a sigh at thought of how soon was effaced from the child-heart the grief that had taken such deep root in his.

One day, he was sitting thus, watching Axel arrange his soldiers for a great parade, when sister Elsie, with a push, struck the whole regiment to the ground. Axel cried loudly, and was in the act of punishing the breach of peace, but immediately repented, and exclaimed:

"That's nothing! I forgive you, little sister. Mamma said I must love you, and I do. I shall always be kind to you."

The thought of his mother brought a shade of sadness over his face. After some silence, he suddenly turned to the father, and said:

"Papa, do you long as much as mamma did to go to Jesus?"

The question was so unexpected, and sounded so strangely to the merchant's ear, that he could give no answer, and felt quite distressed before the child. To say "Yes," he knew too well would be an untruth; and from a negative, his

4

heart recoiled. His answer, therefore, became an evasive question.

"Why do you ask me this, my boy?"

"Well, I was thinking how beautiful it must be there; and it would be the very best thing, if we could all live there together. Mamma sometimes read to me about heaven. How is it that it stands in the Bible about the white clothes, and all the beautiful things?"

"I don't know quite how it stands," replied the father, yet more confused by the boy's question. "You must ask Aunt Lena about it. I have no time to sit here longer. Good-bye, little ones."

With redoubled zeal, he now engaged in business, hoping thereby to divert his mind, not only from grief, but from certain questions that began to stir within him.

Earth, with its multitudinous cares, had, until now, wholly engrossed his attention; yet he was no skeptic. No, he acknowledged that quite surely there must be one who was "The Most High," an arranging, ruling power, guiding the destinies of men and measuring the courses of the stars, but to whom he, the individual, felt so small and foreign, that although, indeed, full of awe, he bowed before him in the distance, he felt no desire to approach him.

Now arose the question, Was his belief faith?—
the faith that enabled his wife, with a smile of
hope, to meet death; that spoke in the quiet
look with which his sister contemplated life;
that sounded so pleasantly from the lips of his
child, as it folded the little hands in prayer, and
then slumbered so sweetly, as if in consciousness that the blessing prayed for rested over it.
No! Their relationship to God must be quite
different from that in which he stood to him;
but this was natural. Could he feel like a
woman or a child? He, who, from earliest
youth, had been accustomed to rely upon himself, and, through his own diligent efforts, had
attained an independent and honorable position
in society—had he not full right to an inner
independence? Reason and self-righteousness
answered: "Yes; the weak may pray for grace;
to the strong, it were more becoming to try to
earn it. Live on, blameless as ever. Perform
thy duty as well as thou canst. God demands
not more of thee." Thus he reasoned, endeavoring, on false foundations and crooked conclu-
sions, to rear a structure inside whose walls he
could escape the voice of God.

Lena surmised that the struggle was begun
in her brother's heart, and longed to reach
out to him a helping hand; but, whenever she

sought to engage him in conversation suited to
this purpose, his replies were so short and evasive as to cause her to retire from the effort,
understanding that he was unwilling to open his
heart to her, and fearing, by unseasonable conversation, to do more harm than good. She
had been brought to believe without seeing, and
now, in faith, submitted into the hands of the
Lord her care for the spiritual welfare of her
brother, praying for him and for herself that
grace might be given her so to live as to cause
no hinderance or stumbling-block upon his path.

Chapter V.

SUMMER IN THE COUNTRY.

THUS quietly to the members of the Stark household did the years pass away. Industry and order pervaded the home, and the spirit of prayer rested over it.

Unweariedly, in all respects, did Lena watch over the children confided to her care and protection; and her efforts were crowned with success. No one could show a finer, healthier boy than was Axel, when, after the expiration of six years, again we see him, with blooming cheeks and a look so open and honest as to cause one to feel that no falsehood has ever compelled him to drop his eye. We will not assert that he, although a knight without fear, was always without reproach. That his Viking inclination led him into many adventures not agreeing with the precepts of school discipline, nor his aunt's admonitions concerning his clothes, we are forced to acknowledge; for pants, blouses, and caps spoke for themselves.

As to Elsie, we may consider her as a new acquaintance. The little tottering babe is now a fine, light-haired, blue-eyed girl of seven, graceful in every movement.

Lena we find again, untouched by time, as erect and diligent as six years before. Perhaps the years have sprinkled a little more silver in her hair; but, if so, no one notices it.

It is Spring, at least according to the Almanac, when we make this visit to merchant Stark.

Axel has just concluded a lively description of a school-recess battle, with snow-balls, and other masculine feats, which, to a less heroic comprehension, would seem pretty nearly allied to street fights.

Elsie, although full of admiration for the courage of her brother, ventured to remark:

"Fie! to be always fighting so much!"

"O, there is no harm in it," replied Axel.

"Yes; it is unchristian," said Elsie, looking wise.

"No, indeed, it is n't," replied Axel. "It belongs to the duties of a Christian school-boy to teach his comrades morals. If any one behaves foolishly, he must be punished. You must n't think me such a rooster as to do all I can to get into a fight. No; if I fight, it is either for honor or duty!'' and, as he spoke, the fun beamed so from his eyes that even Aunt Lena could not preserve her gravity, although she shared not in his opinion of the Christian fight.

''That you fight for honor when you throw snowballs, I can partly understand,'' said she; ''but when does duty impel you to do so?''

''O, that is n't so seldom,'' replied Axel. ''When I see a big boy attack a little one, or when Will Asp plagues the cats, and such things.''

''And do n't you try to talk with them when they do so?'' asked his aunt,

''Sometimes,'' replied Axel; ''but then they only tease me, and call me the protector.''

''And then you flog them, do you, from a pure sense of duty, and without desire for revenge?'' continued the aunt.

''Yes, I have believed so. Perhaps I was mistaken,'' replied Axel. ''I shall think about it more carefully next time.''

And, to avoid further questioning, he sprang up and drew Elsie with him, declaring that she certainly needed a little exercise.

The same day, at dinner, Mr. Stark remarked that he had purchased a place in the country.

"Indeed! Are you going to undertake farming?" asked Lena, surprised.

"No," replied the merchant. "It is a very small affair. The whole consists of only two and a half acres, including the garden, three acres of birch wood, a building of four rooms besides the kitchen, and place for two more rooms in the attic."

"Where is it?"

"Beside the Mælar, about three miles from the city. The former owner was in distress for money, and his description of the rural quietness of his little farm induced me to buy it. It will be good for the children out there—myself too—to get a little rest now and then;" and, with an appearance of fatigue, he stroked the thin, light hair over his bald pate.

"Shall we move into the country?" asked Axel, who had been an eager listener to the conversation.

"Yes; aunty and you children will go and live there during the Summer. I shall have to be contented with a visit to you now and then," answered the father. "Some repairs may be necessary, and I think of going out there to-morrow. So, if the weather is fine, may be aunty and you little folks would like to go with me."

An outburst of joy from the children was the response, while even Aunt Lena appeared much pleased with the invitation.

And the weather was fine. The sun shone beautifully bright, as is usual on pleasant days in the beginning of March, when its rays induce tears from the snow and blushes from the birch-trees.

The horses trotted gayly, drawing the capacious wagon which contained our friends through the noisy streets of the city, out upon the country road. The children were amused and enlivened by all they heard and saw on this, their first highly interesting trip. Each insignificant occurrence gave rise to questions and merriment; yet thought and fancy were mostly occupied with the aim of the journey—the new Summer home. It was not without a feeling of disappointed anticipation that they finally stopped before a small, yellow, one-story house, surrounded by stunted gooseberry-bushes, and heard that this was "Larkheim." However, the site was advantageous, the sea near, and the wood—or, rather, the birch grove—handsome. The rooms were dilapidated, but high and airy; and when the children heard of all the improvements to be made by carpenters and painters, and that a gardener living in the vicinity was to

rearrange the garden so as to render it more
deserving the name, they soon saw all in rose-
colored light, and laid happy plans for the
Summer's amusements.

In the latter part of May the little country-
seat was ready, and, in its cozy simplicity,
looked really inviting. Whole, neat, and taste-
ful must every thing be that belonged to merchant Stark—this was necessary to success; but
his indulgence in the luxury of country life must
be in strict frugality.

The costly furniture was left in the city.
Here all was new, but of the simplest character.
The cook was offended; and Miss Lisette, the
housekeeper, could n't understand what Mr.
Stark was thinking about, to bring himself down
to the use of birch furniture, and not have 'a
decent looking-glass in the whole house. Yet
this reproach from the region of the kitchen did
not disturb the enjoyment of the family.

It is Saturday evening, the first one in their
new home. The merchant, with countenance
particularly cheerful, is sitting upon the teeter-
board, under one of the birches, smoking a
cigar; while Lena sits near by, busy at her
knitting, and the children are skipping gayly
around for flowers.

"Do you know, Lena," said the merchant,

"this is the best movement I have ever made. It is a pleasure to see the children enjoying so much freedom, and I feel enlivened, both in body and mind."

"Yes," said Lena, "it is delightful to see the wonders of God in nature. On a pleasant Spring day, like this, there seems, each hour, new cause for grateful adoration."

"You are right," replied her brother. "I confess that, when I concluded to make this purchase, the thought occured to me that here I should come a little nearer God than I have been."

"As Creator, he is certainly more manifest to us here than in the city," said Lena; "but if we know him not as a Savior and Reconciler, our distance from him remains as great as ever."

"Do you think so? I do n't feel that way," said the brother. "When I heard Elsie, this morning, saying 'Our Father,' it made an entirely new impression upon me. 'Our Father!' These are remarkable words. They have sounded in my ears ever since; and, they seem so child-like, I imagine that I hear them repeated in the blending of a thousand voices. Yes; if God is my Father, I would like to know him better than I do. My Sovereign he has always been; but the knowledge of him as such has long been

unsatisfactory. I have carried with me a disquiet that I feared to frame into words. When
shall it become otherwise?"

There was a touching seriousness in this confession, which so unexpectedly had burst from
the chains of many years' silence. Lena placed
her hand upon her brother's arm, and said:

"Believe on the Lord Jesus Christ, and thou
shalt be saved, and thy house."

The merchant made no reply, and silence
ensued. Peace rested over the surrounding landscape. The children, in their search for flowers,
had gone so far away that their voices were no
longer heard. Even the light rustle of the birch
leaves was hardly perceptible. The sea lay
calmly reflecting the deep blue sky of Spring.

Lena felt God's presence, not alone in majesty, as expressed in the grand simplicity of
Scripture, "The Spirit of God moved upon the
face of the waters;" but also near, with its gracious call in the sinful, human heart of her
brother. O, would there the holy word of creation sound, "Let there be light?"

The merchant's head had dropped in thought.
Lena could not see his countenance, but she
knew what was passing in his soul.

Finally he arose, buttoned his coat, saying:

"I believe it is becoming cool. Please call

in the children; they will easily take cold;" and, without looking at Lena, he entered the house.

Thus ended the conversation that awoke such glad anticipations in the patient sister. But let us not judge too hastily.

. Why did the merchant stare away so as he spoke? Was it to hide two tears that strove to make their downward course from behind his spectacles? And why this hurry to enter the house? Can it be that he is taking from his pocket a little worn book, long concealed there as a memento of his wife? Until now it has been to him only a reminder of the departed one; will he now seek therein the well of life? We are not certain; but let us hope. Lena did so.

To the table the children came, with fresh appetites and spirits. They had had a splendid time, and made the most remarkable discoveries. When hunger was appeased, fatigue came, and the time for good-night; but, evidently, there was something that the merchant wished to say. He opened his mouth and shut it again, coughed a little short yet prolonged cough, and began:

"I would wish—I wonder if you would n't like that—we should read a little, before we separate. It seems to me it would be proper to consecrate our new home with an evening prayer."

With joyful emotion, Lena accepted the proposal, and the children became wide awake and
surprised. It was a peaceful, blessed evening
hour—the first of many, many such experienced
there. To Lena it was like the mount of trans-
figuration, and, with the disciples, she was ready
to exclaim, "Lord, it is good to be here." The
merchant bowed humbly. He, too, felt the presence of his Lord and Master; but not as did the
open-hearted Peter, when in holy ecstasy he ventured to speak with his Lord. No; but like the
same Peter at the solemn moment of the call,
when he fell down at Jesus' knees, saying,
"Depart from me; for I am a sinful man, O
Lord!" And as with the fisherman at Gennes-
aret, so was it here. The same voice whispered
to the trembling heart, "Fear not!" Even the
children felt strangely affected. Axel, with his
dark, thoughtful eyes, looked searchingly into
his father's face, as if there to find out what was
passing. Elsie felt that childish rest in the sense
of God's presence, that intuitive conception of
the Holy, pictured by Raphael; but which words
can not represent.

Chapter VI.

THE TUTOR.

O N Monday morning, Mr. Stark returned to the city and his business. After the father's departure, the children were reminded that for them also the working days had begun, wherefore books, slates, and writing materials were taken out.

Elsie's education was as yet in its earliest stage, its guidance wholly the work of Lena, who, like her brother, entertained a real dread of "schools for girls." Axel had already been two years a member of the Clara School, in Stockholm, and considered himself a pretty scientific sort of individual, when before aunt and Elsie his erudition shone.

Now it was arranged, that, during the Summer, the instruction of both Axel and Elsie should be intrusted to a young relative, Thorsten Holt, who had just completed his collegiate course, and who, by the recent death of his father, had made the sad but common discovery, that, instead of being an heir to wealth, he stood in the world alone and poor. Thorsten's father and merchant Stark were cousins, and in early youth had been on terms of particular friendship. Afterward they became separated, not only by distance—Mr. Holt settling in one of the Southern towns of Sweden—but by difference of taste and opinion. While merchant Stark, as well in private as in business life, pursued an even, quiet course, Holt's life resembled a splendid fire-work. He kept a sumptuous establishment, made a brilliant match, large speculations, and—suffered great losses. His wife died early. When himself felt death approaching, and realized in what an unfortunate condition he must leave his only child, his last request to Thorsten was that he should turn to Mr. Stark for advice and assistance. When, therefore, the young man had passed his senior examination, he wrote to this unknown relative, offering, as apology for doing so, his father's dying wish, and stating his design to seek a situation as tutor, to which end, referring to the inclosed certificate, he solicited the recommendation of Mr. Stark. The reply was a friendly invitation to come to the merchant as instructor of his children, and consider their home as his own. The offer was received with gratitude, and Thorsten wrote that he should soon appear.

To prepare themselves for his reception, rather than for work, Axel and Elsie were now busily engaged in arranging their books. Where was to be the study-room was a problem difficult to solve; for the small house contained none that could be spared for this purpose. The chambers had been fitted up as sleeping apartments—one for the merchant, the other for Axel and the expected tutor. Finally, it was decided that the mental should unite with the physical in the use of the dining-room. A table was placed at one of the windows, and a book-shelf in the corner beside it.

The children's share in this arrangement being completed, liberty to roam was again obtained, a hill that arose behind the birch grove being their prescribed limit. An old oak, that had not as yet donned its green Summer dress, with wide-spread arms beckoned them upward for a look around; and, sure enough, it might be worth while to go! The beautiful Mælar Bay lay radiant in the sunshine, whose light presented the changing beauty of the shore in munificent splendor of colors, interrupted here and there by projecting granite rocks and groups of somber needle-trees. Sev-

eral country-seats seemed, in the distance, transformed from stately villas to unpretending cot-
tages. Beyond the hill was seen the broad
turnpike with its equestrians and pedestrians,
and a distance further the sea, upon which
came hissing onward a small steamer, which
took the children's undivided attention. It was
quickly approaching shore, and would certainly
land at their quay, as the children called it,
although the quay was at some distance from
Larkheim, and belonged really to a larger
country-seat in the neighborhood. A steamer
stopped here only in case it contained some
passenger wishing to land, or was signaled to
do so from the shore.

"What if it should be Thorsten Holt who
has come!" exclaimed Elsie.

"We must watch and see who steps ashore,"
said Axel.

The little steamer drew up to the landing,
and a young man wearing the student cap
sprang upon it, carrying with him a hat-case
and valise. A trunk followed, and the steamer
hurried away. There now stood the young
man, looking around, in order to determine
his course and discover some person to carry
his trunk, when his eye fell upon a boy who
was near, fishing.

"Here, boy!" he called; "will you come and help me?"

The boy was quite heedless of the call, hardly bestowing as much as a look in return.

"Would you like to earn some money?" the traveler again shouted.

This call produced a quite different effect from the former. The fishing-rod was laid down, and the young fisherman hastened toward the gentleman, who seemed amused at the eagerness with which the response was made to the offer of money. Human weaknesses were as yet only a study that interested without disturbing him. He saw these in others, rather than in himself, and so could smile at them.

"Can you carry this trunk?" he asked.

"Certainly," answered the boy.

"Can you show me the way to Mr. Stark's country-seat?"

"No; I never heard of such a place."

"Do you know a place called Larkheim?"

"Yes; it's one of the houses over there."

"Indeed! Well, let us start for it, then."

Meanwhile, the children, convinced that the stranger was their expected teacher, descended the hill, and reached the turnpike just as he was passing the birch grove.

On seeing them, he stopped and asked Axel:

"Can you tell me, my boy, which of those places is Larkheim?"

"Yes; it is just this one here," replied Axel.

"Mr. Stark's residence?"

"Yes."

"The little rural cottage there?   Impossible!" said the young man.

Axel blushed, and answered, proudly:

"It is as possible as that I am his son."

"Well! well!   Pardon me, my little relative; I meant no harm.   I only expected to see a different style.   Then you are Axel Stark, and this is little—"

"Elsie," replied the little girl, looking up, timidly.

"Yes, that's the name," continued the young man, "and mine is Thorsten Holt.   I bring you papa's greeting.   I was with him an hour ago."

Axel, who had become a little out of humor at the somewhat depreciative manner in which Thorsten expressed his surprise at the appearance of Larkheim, and, too, entertained an unpleasant suspicion that he had given a pert reply, had gone in advance, under pretense of hastening to Aunt Lena with tidings of Thorsten's arrival.   With the instinct of her sex, Elsie felt that she must say something to efface any impression that may have been produced by Axel's appearance; and, although she could not think of any thing more to offer than "You are welcome!" she spoke in such a childishly hearty manner that the visitor's countenance assumed a look of grateful pleasure which was quite becoming to him.

Thorsten Holt had a prepossessing exterior: there was an elasticity and grace in all his movements that spoke of refined culture, health, and vigor. The features of his face were not really handsome, but harmonized, and produced a good effect. The nose had a certain inclination to lift a little higher than necessary, and always, on doing so, was followed by a smile which some thought ironical, others judged according to their individual conceptions of it; but which, to most persons, was displeasing. He had also another smile, with which all were not familiar— a smile that broke forth like the sun through a cloud, spreading warmth and light. It was this smile that was produced by Elsie's greeting.

"Thank you, little Elsie," he replied. "How old are you?"

"Seven years," was the reply.

"Then I am to teach you the A, B, C?" he continued.

The graduate did not seem to relish the idea of this employment.

"No, sir," replied Elsie, "I can read. I know the little Catechism by heart, and Part First in the big Bible History, and I have studied grammar some."

"O! then you are quite a scholar."

"Axel knows much more than I do," continued the child. "He has so many books! Some of them even aunty has never read, and she is so old!"

"Does aunty read much?" asked Thorsten.

"Not so very much," replied Elsie. "She reads the Bible every day, and the papers, and she reads, too, in some thick books that I do n't know the names of; I only know that the reading in them is about God."

"O, is she of that kind?" said Thorsten, merrily; but it must not be supposed that the exclamation was one of satisfaction.

They had now arrived at the house, and were received by Aunt Lena, who thought, not without a certain disquiet, of the little attic chamber, when she saw the elegant young man.

The rural home, however, produced a better impression on the mind of Thorsten than he had anticipated It was so unlike the home of his childhood, where all was brilliant and imposing, but order and comfort were wanting.

Of his mother he had no recollection. In

his home he had been more as a guest than as
a child. Now here, now there, he had been
sent for education, and only occasionally in the
year, a few weeks at a time, had he been with
his father, whose house was managed by a pas-
sionate housekeeper.

To be sure, Lena at first seemed to him
somewhat reserved; but soon he learned how
much good will and kindness dwelt inside the
stiff exterior. Thorsten, like so many young
people, had a panical dread of the so-called '
"religious;" but, to his surprise, he found in
Lena a character, intelligent, cheerful, and quiet,
quite unlike the compound of sugar and vinegar
of which he imagined the leading features of a
religionist were composed. Sure it was that,
whenever a careless jest was passing his lips, it
stopped half-way, on meeting her earnest look;
and, queerly enough, at such a time, he would
feel vexation with himself, and not at her.

From the first moment, Elsie felt called upon
to stand as arbiter between Thorsten and Axel,
who was often angered by the satirical fun of
the former, and, in his upwelling vehemence,
wanted little of giving vent to his emotions, as
he did among his comrades, in a palpable way.
Her pleasant, complying manners often chased
from Thorsten's countenance the scornful smile,

producing there, instead, a something resembling sunshine, and which exerted over Axel, too, its magical influence, causing him to forget his injuries, and listen to Elsie's fervent assurances that Thorsten was "so kind."

When the merchant came at the close of the week, he found, to his pleasure, that Thorsten was quite at home and contented. Yes, even more independently at home than was strictly agreeing with good etiquette, since he could sit in the parlor with his chair tipped, or half reclining upon the sofa, while reading a newspaper—so unlike the merchant, who sat there erect and orderly, as if each moment expecting to hear a photographer call, "Now!" So, when Lena was alone with her brother, he could not help saying:

"Young people did n't use to throw themselves into chairs in such a position when I was young."

"It is long since we were young," answered · Lena. "Times are changed. What is required of youth is quite otherwise than it used to be. To be sure, Thorsten has a habit of sitting in an indifferent manner, and taking various little liberties; but he can render himself most agreeably attentive to others. He is unselfish; and the interest he manifests in the instruction of

the children seems to me so great that I value
him more than I should, if, without these quali-
ties, he were a model of etiquette."

"O, I don't dislike him, and hope it may be
so that I can be as a father to him," replied
Mr. Stark. "May you, Lena, be enabled to lead
him to become a Christian! He is young, and
ought to be much more easily guided than I, a
sinner hardened with age."

"What do you mean?" said Lena.

"I mean, that, when I was here last, I enjoyed precious moments, in which I seemed
near my Savior, but that I return dull and cold,
unable to call back these feelings. I would like
to become a living Christian; but it is too late.
I am spiritually dead," said the merchant, in a
tone of despair.

"Such a feeling is hard to endure," said
Lena; "but, believe me, when it is accompanied by so much disquietude and grief, it is no
sign of death. Don't let distrust get place in
your heart, but haste with your burden to the
only Helper. Think less upon what you feel
than upon the greatness of the grace that is
offered you."

"It is easier to say than to do," was the
reply. "I have not your experience. To be
sure, it has become so with me that I enjoy

listening to God's truth. During the week, I have thought much upon the sermon to which we listened last Sunday; but, when I read myself, or try to pray, my thoughts scatter, and I feel poor and unfit."

"To be allowed to listen to a pure, clear preaching of the Gospel is a great privilege," replied Lena; "but we are too apt to let the word heard carry us away for the moment, rather than penetrate and remain in the heart; and to sit in one's chamber, in prayer and meditation, alone with God and Christ, is no less a privilege than the former. It is in moments thus spent one gets a foretaste of eternal blessedness—the rest in God."

The merchant looked at his sister with surprise and reverence. Her face seemed radiant with a joy so exalted that involuntarily came to his mind what is written of Stephen: "And all that sat in the council saw his face, as it had been the face of an angel." It was long since he had heard these words; and never had he understood them as now.

We will not follow the merchant, step by step, in the experiences through which he had to pass. His path was onward, although the obstacles that beset it often seemed to him too great to be overcome. Nor will we follow the work in the heart of Thorsten, who, in learning to love the peaceful Christian home, was also brought to comprehend the great truth, seemingly so simple, yet of which it is so difficult to conceive, that life without God, however brilliant and eventful it may appear, is in reality poor and void; while, on the contrary, a life hid with Christ in God is rich and satisfying, however uneventfully it may pass.

It was with regret, when Autumn came, that the family left their Summer resort to go to Winter quarters, in the elegant house in the city. Even the cook and Miss Lisette had found that the country has its charms, although they missed there the large mirrors, and other advantages of civilization.

Thorsten was to return to Upsala, to enter upon his law course. The separation from his new friends cost his feelings more than, in his sense of dignity as a man and student, he was willing to manifest. This was to be his first leave-taking of a real home.

On the evening before his departure, he sat listening to the wailing of the Autumn wind, which fell upon his ear as an accompaniment to his thoughts. His eyes had in this place, for the first time, been opened to view life in its true light. He must leave the quiet freedom

here, and go out alone amid the struggle of life.
Here he had friends; but would he not, when
away, be soon forgotten? His heart needed
them; but they were so happy without him!
He was unnecessary—alone! alone! At this
moment he felt a little caressing hand upon his
arm. It belonged to Elsie, who stood there
looking at him, her bright eyes filled with tears.

"Why are you so sad?" said he, drawing her
tenderly toward him.

"Because you are going to leave us to-morrow," she replied.

"God bless you, little one! Shall you miss
me, when I am gone?" said Thorsten.

"Yes, much; but you will come again on
Christmas, will you not? O, that will be so
nice, so nice!" said the little girl; and hope
shone through her tears.

"I do n't know whether I may," answered
Thorsten, looking at the merchant, who sat regarding them over the top of his newspaper,
which he now let drop in surprise, as he said:

"What do you mean? Have I not, from
the time of our first meeting, told you to consider my home as your own? Do you know so
little of me as to suppose that I do not mean
what I say? It was my earnest intention that
you should do so, before ever I had seen you;

and certainly, now, when you have become dear to us all, it is no less my wish that none of us should remember otherwise than that you have always belonged to us."

Thorsten sprang to his feet with a violence that was dangerous to chairs and tables, and embraced the merchant with a strength that almost alarmed him.

"Thanks! thanks! my boy!" said he. "Let us now speak calmly of the future. Of course, you will spend the Christmas season with us, as also all your other vacations. Axel will have to go into school again; and as to Elsie, I think to have a daily governess for her while we are in the city. Here in the country, I will have no stranger; so, during the Summer months, I depend upon your assistance with both children."

While the merchant was speaking, he had adjusted his spectacles and composed himself from the effect of the embrace; but need we add that he was now again exposed to a similar eruption of gratitude?

Chapter VII.

LEARNED, AND YET IGNORANT.

AGAIN we let some years roll by ere seeking our friends, and shall only cast a brief glance at what has transpired during this time.

After Thorsten had taken his final examination, he obtained a situation as secretary in the employ of the Government, and took up his abode in Stockholm, where he added to the occupation mentioned the tutorship of the Stark family. After the lapse of two years spent there, he was surprised by a letter from a friend of his father, a judge in Schonen, proffering him a position as colleague. He wrote: "I think, in a few years, to retire, and rest upon my laurels. The vacation I shall ask for will be a lasting one. If I find you efficient in your vocation, and we agree, I shall do. my best to have you appointed my successor. As you know, I am an old bachelor, with no one

for whom to accumulate, so you can rest assured
that my stipulations are not severe."

Thorsten's emotions, as he read this letter,
were far from unmixed. He had to acknowledge that the offer was both advantageous and
honorable; but the thought of leaving Stockholm and his home, of exchanging the life he
was leading there for the society of an aged and
probably fretful bachelor, was far from agreeable.
However, concerning the acceptance of such an
offer there could be no question. Axel had
reached his eighteenth year, and was soon to
enter the Upsala University, while the instruction of Elsie, who was now thirteen, one would
justly suppose ought to be resigned to a more
appropriate guide than the young secretary of
twenty-five.

So he accepted, and took his departure,
leaving behind much void, and carrying with
him a rich harvest of pleasant recollections.

The year following, Axel came home from
Upsala, wearing the long-wished-for university-
cap. Full of happiness, he depicted to his aunt
and sister the new life upon which he had
entered.

"But, after all," remarked Elsie, "the best
best part of the life at the University is the
beautiful singing there."

"I do not deny the power of that," said Axel; "but it is not the best part of student life for me. No; I have found a higher aim for my love. It is the world of truth, light, reason, whose treasures entice me with an allurement I can not describe."

"Be careful, Axel, that you are not enticed to idolatry. Make no search for light and truth that draws you away from Him who has said, 'I am the way, the truth, and the life,'" said his aunt, seriously, almost sternly.

'Am I not a Christian? It is just the sense of assurance that I stand upon firm ground that gives me courage to defy a world, if necessary," said Axel, with a look of enthusiasm and presumption.

By his auditors he was regarded with feelings of an opposite character. Elsie looked upon him with one of exultation, bordering upon devotion. He seemed to her as a hero in the cause of Christianity; a martyr, ready to offer his life for his faith. In fancy, she saw him with the saintly halo around his head. Lena, on the contrary, with her knowledge of the human heart, shook her head, and said:

"Let him who thinketh he standeth take heed lest he fall."

"Aunt," exclaimed Axel, "what have I

said that could cause the disapproval you imply?"

"Your words arouse a feeling of anxiety, rather than disapproval," replied the aunt.

"What!" said Axel, "do you think that search and science can hurt the Christian religion?"

"No, my dear," replied the aunt; "to Christianity I see no peril. 'Heaven and earth shall pass away, but my words shall not pass away,' says the Lord, and his words endure forever; but I fear that your thirst for knowledge may induce you to go seeking after broken cisterns that can hold no water, to leave the simplicity in Christ and become absorbed in mere human subtilties."

"Aunt, do you think the simplicity of Christ consists in ignorance and folly?" asked Axel, with warmth.

"No; be it far from me, such a thought," replied his aunt. "A living, progressive faith is already here upon earth—progressive, from one degree to another; but we must seek the wisdom from above in the light of the revealed Word, not in human thoughts or conceits."

Axel had no desire to lay down arms; yet he was silenced, more from esteem to the speaker than from conviction.

6

Lena's apprehension was often aroused during the Summer, although lulled whenever she looked into Axel's clear, honest eyes, whose expression inspired so much confidence in the sincerity and, as she would fain hope, firmness of his character. With earnestness and fervency he participated in their daily devotions, and zealously assisted Elsie in her plans for the extension and improvement of the garden. Now he was his aunt's own precious boy, and she reproached herself for her fears; but then came some shadow or another in the form of infidel writings, in the perusal of which she found him absorbed.

At first she tried advice and warning; but the resistance which he offered was determined. "One has no right to judge without hearing. I will penetrate each nook of this labyrinth of infidelity, so as to be able to repulse the lie," he proudly answered. So she retired, and kept her anxieties to herself, not even communicating them to her brother, as he seemed himself to perceive no peril; and, besides, she felt sure that, were she to acquaint him with her observations and consequent fears, his efforts to influence Axel would prove as fruitless as were her own.

When Axel returned from Upsala, to spend

his second Summer vacation, the shadows had grown. Now, even Elsie began to suspect something wrong. Expressions that aroused her anxiety often escaped her brother. He spoke of "what a one-sided and narrow-minded religion was preached by the ministers; how unfavorably it compared with the newer teaching, in which was found freedom of thought and enlightenment." He read much; with a zeal that was almost feverish, devouring one work of rationalism after another. During family worship he seemed either absent-minded, or, if otherwise, disapproving remarks concerning what he had heard were the consequence, giving rise to grave dispute.

After such conversation, his aunt looked so care-worn, and Elsie so frightened, that Axel resolved to fetter his frankness, and endeavor, as far as possible, to avoid wounding their feelings; yet looked down with compassion upon poor, weak minds who lacked his strength for rising upward on strong wings to the liberty of thought that gave him so much satisfaction. If only he could rise a trifle higher, so that that which was as yet obscure should become clear to him, then it would be his mission to open the porches of Elysium to his family. He thought of how surprised and bewildered they would become, while he should be their prop and leader.

But what thought the father? the reader perhaps may ask. Well, he admired his son's great diligence. Having himself lacked a scientific education, he desired that his son should enjoy, in rich measure, its advantages. He should take his degree, and then freely choose his own future course. The change in him, seen by his aunt and suspected by his sister, almost wholly escaped the attention of his father, who was so happy at having himself found the peace of the Gospel as to render it impossible, to his conception, that children, taught and reared as his had been, could ever leave the faith which was the substance of his hope in life and in death. If, in his father's presence, any word of coldness or indifference were dropped by Axel, the former thought "his poor boy dull and weary from over-exertion in study, and that at heart he was a Christian, as warm as formerly."

Mr. Stark's blindness to his son's condition may seem unnatural; but we must consider how brief were his visits to Larkheim, and how few were his opportunities for observing Axel, in comparison with those of his sister and Elsie. Besides, Axel carefully avoided all religious conversation with his father, desiring not to begin any real contest until quite secure in the use of his weapons; and yet all was not perfectly clear to him.

Chapter VIII.

POISON OF UNBELIEF.

T is in the last of May, the third Spring after Thorsten's departure, when again we enter the Stark home. Larkheim has been much beautified during our absence. Bushes and trees have grown; the grass-plots are tolerably smooth and fine; numerous collections of plants give token of a rich yield of blossoms for the season, although only few of Spring's earliest ones have as yet been able to develop their splendor of color and their fragrance. A veranda has been added to the house, which has been remodeled so as, without disturbing the simplicity of the place, to increase the comfort and satisfy Elsie's sense of beauty. The shade of the birch-trees is, as ever, a favorite resort; so now, too, the coffee-table stands spread there, surrounded by light garden chairs.

Axel is expected, and for his reception Elsie

is engaged in arranging as delightfully as possible. She deems a bouquet is still wanting, wherefore hyacinths, narcissuses, and tulips offer their young lives to fill the void; and, while this is going on, we will seize the opportunity for a look at her.

This finely formed young lady—is she really the same little Elsie whose acquaintance we made in the nursery? Often one looks with a feeling of regret upon a once lovely child who has undergone this change. To be sure, the lineaments are finer, the bearing elegant, the toilet pretty; but where is the expression of gentle innocence? How will Elsie stand the investigation? Let us step nearer. She is just now lifting her head, stroking back the unmanageable ringlets that will not remain in place, and we meet her glance. Give a deep look into those bright, beautiful eyes! There you again find the child, although a faint shade of sadness obscures the usually happy expression. She is thinking of Axel, and wondering how now she shall find him. His letters have been of late so few and brief! Would he in spirit be yet more widely separated from them than when at home last Summer and during the Christmas vacation? He had seemed so happy when they separated, and had said that soon the time would

come when they should understand each other.
Would it be thus? Yes, surely all again would
be well.

The bouquet was ready. It looked so well
there in its place! Elsie was charmed with
the success of her arrangements; and, banish-
ing each sad thought with a smile of hope, she
hastened to the house to call her father and aunt
to share in her admiration.

"Axel must be here immediately," said she.
"See, there he is at the garden gate!"

With an outburst of joy, she flew to meet
him; but she suddenly paused, while a look
of painful surprise drove the bloom from her
cheeks. This emaciated figure; this pallid face,
in which suffering has plowed its deep furrows;
these dark eyes, burning with such a look of
unrest—can it be the promising young student?
He saw the impression his appearance produced,
and, quickly clasping his sister in his arms, exclaimed, with assumed gayety:

"Well, don't you recognize me? You think,
perhaps, that I carry the same inscription as the
baker's goose that had been exchanged in the
night: 'Yesterday I was fat; to-day I am somewhat spare.'"

"Yes," replied Elsie. "What is the matter?
How dreadfully you look!"

"O, see, there are father and aunt! I have n't greeted them yet," said Axel; and, without answering Elsie's question, he turned from her and proceeded toward the veranda, where Mr. Stark and his sister were sitting.

The same anxious question met him there:

"Dear boy, what ails you?"

"O, nothing to speak of. A little rest and quiet will set me right," answered Axel.

In the smothered sigh that escaped with these few words his aunt heard confessed what she had expected.

"That study! that study!" exclaimed the merchant, shaking his head with the well-meant design of hiding from his sister and Elsie what he thought he read in his son's emaciated features.

But Mr. Stark was no actor. His look inquired as plainly as words could have done, "How deeply have you fallen?"

In spite of the balmy Spring air, the fragrance of the flowers, and the inviting aroma of the coffee, the spirits of the company could not be rallied to the festivity anticipated by Elsie on this longed-for day. Each wished to keep his anxiety to himself, and no one succeeded; so, when Axel remembered that he had brought letters and papers from the city, it was an agreeable interruption.

Lena and Axel fortified themselves behind their new periodicals. Elsie read "the marriages and deaths" in the daily papers; and the merchant opened his letters, laying aside one after another without remark, until he came to the last, when, with suprise and no very great satisfaction, he exclaimed:

"This is a tiresome story. Superintendent Billmer writes, asking me, as a favor, to receive his wife, who is coming to Stockholm for the sake of consulting physicians here, procure her comfortable rooms, etc. She is extremely nervous, and unaccustomed to journeying alone. Business prevents him from accompanying her; so he solicits this service of me."

"Poor woman!" exclaimed Elsie, compassionately; "if only we could assist and nurse her!"

"You little innocent!" said Axel; "do you think that a young lady, who can travel alone from Norrland to Stockholm, is so sick as to need you to step forward as a Sister of Mercy?"

"Certainly the letter states that she is sick; does n't it, father?" said Elsie.

"Yes, to be sure, it says that she is coming here for the purpose of consulting the doctors," answered Mr. Stark; "but I think, with Axel, that we need n't infer from this that her health is so very poor. From what I have heard of Mrs. Billmer, she is a great beauty, spending her life in nonsensical pursuit of pleasure. So I fear she would not sympathize much either with aunt or Elsie."

"Then I will be her knight," said Axel. "Of course, she will wish amusement. I will accompany her around, and show her all there is to be seen."

Elsie looked at her brother in surprise. His readiness to become a cicerone was quite unexpected. The aunt looked upon her periodical and sighed. She understood that no feeling of gallantry or kindness had induced from Axel such a remark—only the restless something in his eye, and which so evidently he was trying to conceal from those around him.

The merchant, whose head had been busy with numerous plans for a reasonable opportunity to speak with his son alone, now proposed that he should go to his room and "try some new cigars."

When the two were alone together, the father advanced to Axel, who had taken a seat at the window and was staring at the landscape, and, kindly placing his hand upon his arm, said:

."My poor boy! Tell me the whole truth. What have you upon your conscience?"

There was no reply.

"If you have contracted debt, only mention the amount, and be at rest. I hope I can pay it."

A painful smile overspread Axel's face. A bitter reply was at his lips—what good could all the gold in the world do him?—but his father's sad, loving look kept it back, and he answered :

"I owe nothing. On the contrary, the condition of my purse has been so good as to allow me to lend two of my classmates money for their journeys home. If I look like a criminal, it arises from weariness of mind and body. I have no base act to confess;" and the proud, open look of old met that of the father.

"Thank God!" said the merchant. "You really frightened me. I was afraid you had left your Lord, and suffered the world to entice you into sin."

"Father, I have left him. Concerning my actions, I have answered; but not my belief," said Axel, gloomily. "The Christ whom you adore, and I used to worship, exists no more for me. I found him to be an empty shell, which, with contempt, I have thrown away."

"Unhappy boy!" cried the merchant. "Do you dare to scoff?"

"What have I said?" asked Axel, becoming suddenly paler. "Forget the confession that escaped me, and do n't be the least unhappy on my account, father."

"How could I forget that my child is exposed to fearful peril, both for time and eternity?" answered the father in despair, drying the sweat of anguish from his forehead.

"O, do try to forget!" said Axel, seizing his hand; "and forgive me the pain I cause you. My inability to bear my burden alone is contemptible weakness. I fear that aunt, too, has looked through me, and that I make Elsie unhappy. I darken life to you all by my lack of self-control."

"What can we do for you?" asked the father. "Can not we convince you that—"

"No! no! Spare me the pain your efforts would give me! Perhaps my answers would awaken in your mind, also, the doubts that darken my existence," replied Axel.

"But I have one weapon with which to combat your enemies. You can not deny me the use of this," said the father, with a ray of hope in his eyes. "I can pray for you."

Axel was affected, and kissed his father's hand. He was too enlightened to believe in the power of prayer; yet the young skeptic, the denier of the highest love, was moved by the loving care of his earthly father.

The anxiety that the emaciated, suffering appearance of Axel awakened in those around him gave rise to many serious conversations and deliberations between the merchant and his sister. That the cause of his suffering was a mental one, there was no doubt. Axel had himself acknowledged this in his conversation with his father, although afterward he evaded any reference to the subject, and, with an assumed appearance of cheerfulness, attempted to conceal the dark condition of his mind.

But not alone mentally did he suffer. His physical system reeled under the burden of the mental, and it became daily more evident that neither the salubrious air nor the repose at Larkheim was sufficient to renew his vigor or appetite. The anxious father consulted with his physician, who suggested "sea-bathing and sea-air." Axel showed no inclination to follow the doctor's recommendation of a journey to the western coast, and, when the matter was proposed, only replied, half jestingly:

"I don't go unless Elsie goes with me. When I am alone with her, my gloom will sometimes recede, and life lose some of its heaviness."

"Elsie can't go without your aunt," replied the merchant.

"O father," said Axel, "I should never be willing to have aunt leave you for my sake; so the matter is decided. I shall stay at home."

"But the journey is necessary to the restoration of your health, perhaps the preservation of your life," pleaded the father.

"O, no," replied Axel. "The whole North Sea couldn't wash away my scruples; and they alone depress me."

What was to be done? To persuade Axel, dejected and ill as he was, to travel alone, seemed greatly objectionable; and Elsie could not go without female protection. The merchant sighed, and Aunt Lena appeared uneasy; but nothing was decided upon.

Chapter IX.

HONEY UPON THE LIPS—WORMWOOD IN THE HEART.

LETTER had been sent to Norrland, inviting Mrs. Billmer to make the house of Mr. Stark her home during her sojourn in Stockholm, and now we find all in readiness for her reception. The city residence, which recently had been closed for the season, is open again to light and air. Elsie has arranged fresh flowers in the vases, and the tea-machine is already singing in the dining-room. All is in readiness, and Elsie beginning to be impatient and wonder if they never are coming; while Aunt Lena, in her old-fashioned but faultless brown silk, and sedate-looking-cap, moves about with a look of anxiety, and a little more erect than usual, now taking a peep into the kitchen, now visiting the guest-chamber, to see that all is in readiness there.

Finally, a carriage stops, and the expected guest has arrived, accompanied by Mr. Stark and Axel, who both have been out some distance to meet her.

Mrs. Billmer was a pale, fine-looking person, with large, lively brown eyes, beaming with the fire that flames, flashes, and sometimes burns, but never warms. To ask for her age were a breach of etiquette; so we will content ourselves in supposing that she is between thirty and forty. With nervous vivacity she embraced Elsie, bowed condescendingly to Lena, complimented Mr. Stark, looked at Axel, and gave directions to her maid.

Elsie was surprised and charmed. Lena's mind was overcast with clouds. Mr. Stark felt distressed and awkward at the expressions of gratitude showered upon him; while Axel alone seemed quite self-possessed and ready to engage in lively conversation, although his cheerfulness was of the same joyless nature as at the time of his return from Upsala, when, for a while, he tried to tear himself from his gloom. Mrs. Billmer, however, was an observer too superficial to suppose him otherwise than a happy, merry individual.

After a while, Elsie gathered courage to participate in the conversation; but more than once blushed with a sense of inefficiency in this kind of entertainment. Mrs. Billmer's conversation

fluttered around in a sphere quite foreign to
Elsie, whose life had glided onward within the
quiet—many, perhaps, would say narrow—pre-
cinct of home.

Lena felt it her duty to protect Elsie, as far
as possible, from what might prove detrimental
to her inner life. It was the aunt's conviction
that, as necessary as is pure atmosphere to the
physical well-being of the child, is it to the development of its character that the moral atmosphere it breathes should be as pure as is possible here amid the contagion of sin. To be sure,
she knew that no cloister walls shut out the
world, and that life is fraught with impurity;
but why seek peril? The child-mind is so sus-
ceptible to impressions that we of maturity must
shudder could we see how many a thoughtless
word, dropped from our lips upon the ear of
childhood, has taken root in the heart, sprung
up, and borne fruit a hundred-fold. How vain
are all our efforts to keep children from contact
with sin! But shall we, then, be less watchful
to protect them against exterior evil? Ought we
not to endeavor to have the good seed as unmixed as possible with what is otherwise? The
enemy neglects not to sow tares.

Lena had practiced with Elsie no strict rules
and prohibitions; but, by a gentle influence, had

led her to feel the joy of a higher life than that which is empty and vain. The thought had never occurred to Elsie that, by not participating in certain amusements which from her childhood she had been taught to think objectionable, she suffered any disadvantage. A transient feeling of wonder now arose within her, a curiosity to taste the forbidden fruit. She was ashamed of herself that it should be there, and hastened to drive it away; but was it therefore vanquished?

Mrs. Billmer began, with a suspicious, half-contemptuous look, to regard Lena, who rattled her knitting-needles a little impatiently, and seemed dissatisfied. She had great desire to let drop some subtle remark upon one-sided and narrow-minded views, but deemed it more expedient to recline upon the sofa and feel enfeebled. This movement became the signal for decampment, and soon the little company was separated for the night.

When Mrs. Billmer was alone with her maid, her lassitude seemed in a great measure to disappear. She stretched herself upon a sofa, and began:

"Well, Fanny, is n't it charming to think we are in Stockholm? although it certainly is a trial to have to play the agreeable toward that old dromedary of a merchant, and live under the same roof with his estimable sister. I can't endure her. She seems to disapprove all I say; but one must use self-control. There is some advantage in living gratuitously, the money will go farther; and, besides, the young people are quite agreeable."

"This is a religious family," said Fanny; "the cook told me so."

"Yes, I could see that," replied the lady. "That most worthy aunt looked as if she could have exterminated me; but, if I set about doing so, I can charm her as well as the rest. Yes; now, I have a mind to try. There would be more fun in doing so than in submitting to such looks of disapprobation as were cast upon me when I was talking of this and that with the young people;" and, with a merry laugh, she sprang from her indolent posture, and resigned herself to the care of Fanny.

Soon the pretty maid was ready, with a courtesy, to ask:

"Is there any thing more I can do for you, madam?"

"No. Good-night, Fanny."

Next morning, as Lena was alone in the breakfast-room, waiting for the family to convene, she was pleasantly surprised by the sweetest "Good-morning!" so utterly unlike the cold

"Good-night!" bestowed upon her the evening before. In an affectionate, amiable manner, Mrs. Billmer caught hold of both Lena's hands, and, looking beseechingly, exclaimed:

"O Miss Stark! how glad I am to find you alone, that I may relieve my heart of what has rested so heavily upon it ever since last night! I saw that I displeased you. I spoke in such a thoughtless, frivolous manner! I know I must have seemed to you vain and superficial; but I have lacked the loving care that protects Miss Elsie from all contact with the follies of society. I can not help regarding her with a feeling almost of envy. I look at her, and wish I were as innocent. Forgive me!"

Lena was struck. Her conscience accused her of having judged Mrs. Billmer pretty severely, so she earnestly apologized for having formed of her a rash opinion; and her straightforward truthfulness caused a fickle repentance in the fair hypocrite. It might have been a more enduring one had she allowed herself to listen to its voice; but she quickly silenced conscience with the convenient consolation that she had meant no harm.

Mr. Stark, Elsie, and Axel entered. Their appearance, too, was not the same as on the previous evening. The merchant was less reserved. Axel, who, on the contrary, seemed to have forgotten his fine intention to render himself agreeable and interesting, was silent and retiring.

Elsie was dejected. No one knew what a long, long time in the night she had lain awake, thinking and wondering about the varieties of pleasure in society, moving so close around her, and of which she knew nothing yet so much desired a glimpse. Then, in the stillness of the hour, she saw all in its true charater, and a sense of this depressed her.

Mrs. Billmer displayed less vivacity than on the evening previous, having decided upon an appearance more subdued. Lena was regarded by her as already conquered. It was the merchant against whom now she turned her weapons; and, knowing that the quickest, surest way to the father's heart is in speaking of his children, with an ability that showed much practice she maneuvered so as to stand alone with the merchant, and, in the distance regarding Axel and Elsie with a look of tender sadness, exclaim:

"O Mr. Stark, what an interesting, intelligent appearance your son has!"

"I could wish he appeared more healthy, and less interesting," replied the father. "His look gives me great anxiety. He needs a trip to the western coast; but he obstinately refuses to go without Elsie, and, of course, she can not go alone with him."

The western coast was the aim of Mrs. Bill-mer's desires and plans. A new idea flashed into her mind. Good companionship was a great advantage, and if she could get Axel and Elsie with her, she could render them useful to her.

"But," said she, "if Miss Elsie could go under the protection of an elder lady friend, would it not then be right to comply with his wish, particularly if there should be in Elsie any predisposition to disease? Their mother died of lung disease, did she not?"

"Yes; but there is nothing of that kind the matter with Axel; and Elsie has never been sick since she got through teething," replied the father.

"Perhaps she never has been sick; but she is certainly a tender plant that needs to be well propped," said the lady.

"What do you mean, my dear Mrs. Billmer?"

"Is it possible that sea-bathing has n't been ordered for her too?"

"We have never consulted a doctor concerning her; nor has she any suspicion that her health is otherwise than excellent," replied Mr. Stark.

Here Mrs. Billmer assumed a look of prophetic doubt, and, as if gazing back upon a long
row of sick-beds and death-beds, continued:

"I am no doctor, but I have much experience, and have found that, where there is cause
for fearing hereditary lung disease, too much
precaution can not be used. Look at your
daughter! Is that dejected expression natural?"

"Elsie is pale to-day," replied the father.
"Is it possible that she is in danger? If so, all
obstacles to the journey must be removed.
Axel must make no objection to leaving me
alone. My sister must accompany them."

"Would that be really necessary," said Mrs.
Billmer, modestly. "I know very well that I
can not fill the place of Miss Stark; but in all
probability I shall be ordered to Marstrand.
My whole nervous system is affected to a de-
plorable degree; and, if your lovely daughter
were submitted to my care, I should be most
happy in the opportunity to watch over her
with the tenderest care."

"I thank you," said Mr. Stark; "but—"

"O, I will do it so willingly! But I may
seem unfit to undertake such a charge," interrupted Mrs. Billmer.

"O, certainly not!" said Mr. Stark, bowing,
but exceedingly puzzled.

Mrs. Billmer seized his hand and pressed it.

"Promise me," said she, "not to reject my proposal too quickly. It deserves consideration."

And it was considered. All reasons, *pro* and *con*, were carefully weighed, and the result was that Mrs. Billmer was victorious.

Yet with Lena it cost much struggle to yield Elsie to the care of Mrs. Billmer; for, notwithstanding the touching penitence of this lady, she very soon could but feel the emptiness of certain religious phrases to which she was occasionally treated by her, and she knew that in her company Elsie would be exposed to hitherto unknown temptations. But Elsie was no longer a child, and could not be treated as such. She must learn to discriminate. Lena hoped that her prayers and labor had not been in vain. Besides, her anxiety for Axel was so great that she felt comfort in the knowledge of Elsie's presence with him.

In resigning Elsie to the care of Mrs. Billmer, even the merchant had his scruples; but they were overcome by the lady's assurances of maternal care and the quiet life they should lead at Marstrand; and, although he had not the most perfect confidence in her professions, he blindly believed in her illness, and saw therein protection against a mingling with society.

But Elsie herself, what were her feelings? A transport, mixed with dread. Now, finally, she was to have a glimpse of the world.

They were to start in a fortnight. Mrs. Billmer herself undertook to dictate the arrangement of Elsie's toilet, which care, taken in connection with that of her own, occupied the greater portion of her time; while the oppressive heat prevented any other pleasure undertakings than a couple of excursions in the beautiful environs of the capital.

Axel was one day rashly merry, the next sunk in gloom. This inconsistency rendered him, in Mrs. Billmer's eye, so interesting that, as one day she expressed herself to Elsie, she thought him "exceedingly charming."

Chapter X.

JOURNEY TO MARSTRAND.

THE day of our travelers' departure for Marstrand was a windy, rainy one, and the steamboat trip from Gothenburg was extremely disagreeable. Mrs. Billmer screamed and cried, and occupied the attention of all who would bestow it. Elsie was pale and frightened, and with her whole heart wished herself at home. The seasickness surrounding her, the heavings of the boat, the pent-up air, every thing inclined her to think, with the hen in one of Hans Christian Andersen's stories, "There is no pleasure in traveling."

Finally the heaving decreased, and the comforting exclamation, "We are there!" infused new life into the sick. Mrs. Billmer's first thought was one of solicitude about her appearance, whether her dress was much wrinkled, etc. Elsie saw with surprise that it was the same with most of the passengers. Was she, then, the only one present who thought of thanking God for the preservation of their lives?

As Elsie stood upon deck, inhaling the pure, bracing sea-air, and viewing the strange aspect of nature around her, she was filled with joyful wonder. The evening sun, breaking forth from behind the heavy clouds, threw a charming luster over sky, sea, and cliffs.

"O, how beautiful!" cried Elsie.

But Mrs. Billmer only declared, that, if she were not anticipating a pleasant time in the society at Marstrand, she should certainly become a hypochondriac by looking at those horrible gray cliffs. However, with all the more interest did she view the numerous bathers, who, enticed by the sunbeams and the approaching steamer, had taken an expectant position, for the purpose of viewing and discussing the passengers.

"Look there to the right," whispered Mrs. Billmer to Elsie. "Well, I don't mean the basket-woman, but that company of gentlemen, of course. They have noticed us! How curious they are! O, there is Lieutenant Nollen! He will certainly recognize me—then my incognito will be gone; but you must remain an unknown dignity. Believe me, Nollen don't sleep to-night without learning your name and how much you weigh."

Elsie was astonished at the thought of such remarkable curiosity.

"Do n't you understand Swedish, dear child," said Mrs. Billmer, laughing, "or are you averse to being weighed? This means only the amount of your fortune."

Axel, who meanwhile had, with Fanny, examined the list of baggage and seen it safely ashore, now came for the ladies; and Mrs. Billmer, taking his arm, sailed forth most exquisitely, while Elsie followed, with thoughts unpleasantly occupied with Mrs. Billmer's conversation, the tone of which was to her as new as it was disagreeable. They had hardly stepped upon shore ere Lieutenant Nollen hastened forward to greet Mrs. Billmer.

"Well, my dear madam, what unexpected luck! How do you do?" said the little lieutenant, endeavoring, by contracting his eye-brows and assuming a certain tone of sadness, to manufacture a look of sympathy.

"Poorly, very poorly," replied Mrs. Billmer; "but I hope that Marstrand will give me back my health."

"How lamentable! Is Mr. Billmer with you?"

"No," replied the lady; "I am alone with these young friends. Miss Stark, Mr. Stark, Lieutenant Nollen."

The presentation well over, the Lieutenant endeavored to make himself interesting to Elsie by inquiring "whether she had been seasick, had visited Marstrand before," etc.; but Mrs. Billmer was unwilling to resign him so soon. A student can have his merits; but what is he in comparison with a military officer? Her step, therefore, became heavy and dragging. Axel became alarmed at the weight upon his arm, and asked:

"Are you ill, Mrs. Billmer?"

"O, pardon me!" replied Mrs. Billmer. "I am so fatigued, so faint! I need support; but you are yourself so weak. Lieutenant Nollen, do please have compassion on me."

Axel would not admit that he was too weak for her support; but, with the sweetest smile, she withdrew her hand from his arm and placed it upon that of the Lieutenant, saying, as she did so:

"Remember, Mr. Stark, that I promised to watch over your health with maternal tenderness."

Axel turned away, with very little gratitude for the maternal tenderness; and, fortunately, Mrs. Billmer soon recovered herself so as to glide forward with her usual grace by the side of the Lieutenant, who favored her with as much information concerning the visitors at the place as could be given in a hurry; and, in return for the pleasing intelligence concerning counts and countesses, barons and baronesses, Mrs. Billmer whispered in confidence that Elsie was heiress to a large and solid fortune, which information was received with apparent interest.

The next day was a pleasant one. The cottage that had been prepared for their accommodation during the bathing season was neat and comfortable, and Mrs. Billmer radiated for a wager with the sun, quite happy at thought of so many grandees and so much rare amusement.

Axel came to the breakfast-table, from an early walk among the mountains, with an appetite so fresh that Elsie, who thought she saw already the return of health and strength, was exultant with joy, and seemed like a twittering bird.

When, in the course of the forenoon, Lieutenant Nollen called, he found the travelers in the best of spirits, and, being himself of a planetary nature, soon reflected the common joy, becoming so jovial that one might be misled to suppose him really an interesting person.

Escorted by the Lieutenant, Mrs. Billmer and Elsie made their appearance upon the park, where, thanks to their little knight's good will and desire for chat, they were noticed with a

certain kind of curiosity, which was observed
by Mrs. Billmer with triumphant pleasure, and,
Elsie thought, friendliness.

With restless zeal, Nollen had run around
speaking about the "charming Mrs. Billmer,"
and the "beautiful heiress, Miss Stark," and
now was as zealous in presenting them right and
left.   Besides, Mrs. Billmer was so fortunate as
to find amid the cream of society her good
friend, Mrs. Colonel D——, whose acquaintance
she had made eleven years before, at Medevi,
and who, although to be sure she had at first
some difficulty in recalling to mind this "dear
friend," with delicate tact made amends for for-
getfulness in especial politeness.

Elsie seemed, with Mrs. Billmer, like a little
yawl beside a schooner in full sail; but many,
who with haughty surprise observed with what
dexterity Mrs. Billmer maneuvered to inflate her
sails, had only smiles and encouragements for
the modest yawl.

The programme for the day was, first, a con-
cert of sacred music in the church, and, afterward, music and fireworks upon the water.

Elsie was glad that the first amusements
which presented themselves were of a nature so
innocent that with a good conscience she could
partake of them.   "These would interest even

aunt," thought she, as with childish rapture she listened to the music, watched the many sailing-boats as they glided past each other, and the hissing rockets as they rushed upward, throwing fitful glares over the whole scene.

When again they were at home, and had bidden adieu to Lieutenant Nollen, Mrs. Billmer asked:

"Well, what do you think of Marstrand?"

"It is charming," exclaimed Elsie.

"An intolerable hubbub," muttered Axel, in a surly manner.

"Axel, how can you say so?" said Elsie. "It has been a splendid day. All are so friendly and kind! I begin to doubt that the world is so bad as one imagines at a distance."

"Yes; you will see that there is much that is n't so dangerous as you have supposed," said Mrs. Billmer, in a tone of gayety.

"And much that is more dangerous than you have supposed," said Axel, gloomily, and added, in a whisper: "Beware of letting the first doubt gain entrance! You can not surmise how short the distance is therefrom to hell. Good-night!" and he hurried out.

Elsie stood shocked, and the happy reminiscences of the day seemed to vanish like a bursting soap-bubble; but after a while Mrs.

8

Billmer's chat brought her to her senses again; and, although she fell asleep with a sigh, it was for her brother's sake only.

Mrs. Billmer soon found herself mistaken in having thought Axel an attentive cavalier, of whose time and patience she might freely dispose. With loathing, he retired from the gay social life that surrounded her, spending the greater part of the day upon the water, alone with a silent sailor and his own unhappy thoughts; but what Axel was not, Lieutenant Nollen was all the more willing to become.

"How good-natured and accommodating he is!" exclaimed Elsie, as Lieutenant Nollen hastened away to perform an errand for Mrs. Billmer.

"Fie! what tiresome expressions!" replied Mrs. Billmer. "He is an exceedingly interesting and well-mannered young man, who does n't think upon himself and his own pleasure exclusively, but has thought and sympathy for others; and this you only call good-natured and accommodating!"

Elsie blushed, and turned a look of alarm upon Axel, wondering how he would receive the hint; but he sat there with arms crossed, staring into space, silent and abstracted as before. She felt relieved that he had not been wounded by the insinuation. But would not an outburst of passion have been good for him? Yes, far preferable to this oppressive silence. She must try to waken him from his dreams; and, tenderly laying her hand upon his arm, she asked:

"Are you going out sailing, to-day?"

"Yes," said he, "at eleven o'clock. Perhaps it is time to go;" and, looking at his watch, he found it was eleven o'clock.

"But shall you always go alone? Will you not let us go with you?" asked Elsie.

"To-day it is too windy," was the reply.

"And, besides, we have no time," interrupted Mrs. Billmer. "We are going visiting."

Axel left without a word, or a feeling of regret at the loss of their society. Hardly had he left the door, when Lieutenant Nollen hurried in, panting and smiling.

"Here, my ladies," said he, "I have succeeded in procuring you reading—a French novel; and here are Stockholm papers—*The Day's News* and *New Illustrated Papers*."

"Thank you, my good Lieutenant Nollen," said Mrs. Billmer; "I am quite delighted. Elsie .and I were speaking of how much we are indebted to you."

"Should I be allowed to present a claim, it

would be to demand the glittering reward of a dance with each of you ladies at the *soirée* to-night."

"This I can not give," replied Elsie, blushing.

"How?" inquired the Lieutenant. "Am I already too late? Are you engaged for every dance?"

"No, not at all; but I do n't intend to go to the *soirée;* and, besides, I never dance."

"Why?"

"I disapprove of dancing," replied Elsie, trying to appear calm and firm; but, when her look met the scornful smile of Mrs. Billmer, she felt her courage fail, and tears already trembled in her long dark eyelashes.

"O, my dear," said Mrs. Billmer, "do n't say that you disapprove of dancing. Rather say straight out, 'Aunt do n't allow me to dance.' I shall tell you, Lieutenant, that 'aunt' is a very estimable person, who, until now, has assumed to be conscience for Elsie, and relieve her of all trouble of judging for herself what is right and wrong; but, my dear Elsie, it is really high time that you should for once endeavor to have an opinion of your own. How can you be so unjust as to condemn what you have never seen? Think what an inconsistency! She has never seen a ball."

"Ah! is it possible!" exclaimed the Lieutenant, sympathetically.

"Yes," said Mrs. Billmer; "and it is certainly our duty, as her friends, to resist the prejudice."

Elsie looked down, struggling with herself to keep back the tears which she was unwilling to have seen; and Mrs. Billmer, interpreting her silence as compliance, said, patting her kindly:

"I see that you will not be selfish; so you will go with us to the *soirée*. If you find dancing as dangerous as you have been taught, I shall not ask you to go again. 'One time is no time,' as you know."

"But I neither can nor will dance," said Elsie.

"Well," said Mrs. Billmer, "the less you will risk. To sit and look awhile at us poor children of the world can not be so perilous, I should think."

And Elsie yielded. To sit and look only at the dancing seemed to her really innocent. It might, too, be interesting to see how people of intelligence could find pleasure in such folly. Yes; and when Lieutenant Nollen, with untiring persistency, entreated that she would be his partner only in one little gallopade, encircled by his arm, transported with the music, she glided gracefully away in the dance. When it was over, she remarked:

"I got along better than I expected."

"And was n't it pleasanter, too?" whispered the Lieutenant, looking full into her eye, as he withdrew his arm.

Elsie blushed, but answered, truthfully:

"Yes."

Mrs. Billmer heard the acknowledgment, and laughed triumphantly. However, she made no remark, but hastened to present Baron S——, who requested of Elsie her hand in the next waltz.

"I thank you, I never waltz," replied Elsie, frightened at being unable to say, "I never dance."

"The next *française*, then?"

"I can not dance *française*."

"Indeed! only gallopades? or is Lieutenant Nollen the only fortunate man?"

"Are you crazy, girl?" whispered Mrs. Billmer. "If you have begun to dance, you must go on, or you will make yourself ridiculous."

Then, addressing the Baron, she continued:

"If your grace will have patience with the little nun's ignorance of the mysteries of the *française*, of course she will be very grateful."

"Is it really so?" said the Baron to Elsie.

"Yes, thank you?" answered Elsie, blushing and confused.

Thus, without exactly knowing how it had

After the Ball.

taken place, Elsie found herself transformed from a quiet spectator of the dance to an animated participator in it, and listened with surprise, but not without pleasure, to the flattery to which she was treated. To be sure, the moral atmosphere in which she had been educated was too pure, and the character of her mind too healthful, to deem much of the conversation to which she listened otherwise than insipid and superficial; but, on the other hand, she was too unsophisticated to know that many a worn-out phrase came not from the heart.

"To-day you have done me honor," said Mrs. Billmer, pressing the hand of Elsie, as she wished her good-night.

When Elsie had reached her room, she threw herself, fatigued and excited, upon a sofa. The window stood open, admitting the mild evening air, with a flow of moonshine, which, with its subdued luster, lighted the room. A shudder passed through Elsie. Why did all look so solemn and grave? The peaceful stillness around her harmonized little with the various shades of the unquiet thought and emotion that were moving within her.

There lay the Bible open, as she had left it in the morning without finishing the chapter which she had begun to read. Ought she not to finish it, and end the day, as she was wont, with prayer, and meditation upon God's Word? No; it was sinful to read with thoughts so scattered. She was too tired; and, laying aside the Bible, she shut the window and hastened to bed. She tried to collect her mind for prayer, and found words; but they were cold and lifeless, and drowned by the tones of the dancing-music still resounding in her ear.

Soon she fell asleep, when her thoughts and emotions took the form of fantastic dreams. Now she was surrounded by the changing scenes of the ball, dancing, and listening to the voice of flattery; now surprised by the reproving glances of the moon, which, with Aunt Lena's eyes, looked down from the vault above upon her and her neglected Bible; but then came Mrs. Billmer, illuminated by a big chandelier, assuring her that it was not as dangerous as she supposed, when the moon withdrew behind the clouds, and the music again resounded so enchantingly!

Chapter XI.

"MIT LIF ER EN VAG."
(My life is a wave.)

ELSIE awoke in the morning, tired and depressed. The reproving voice of conscience could not be silenced, although again and again she repeated the words of Mrs. Billmer, "It is not so dangerous." However, she resolved that no one should perceive her feelings concerning the previous evening's amusement.

At breakfast, Axel was somewhat social and attentive, and related incidents of his day previous upon the sea: how he had been induced to sail to Blaakulla, and there had made a pedestrian excursion. On the return home, there had been so little wind that it was one o'clock at night before they reached Marstrand.

"I hope my absence caused you no anxiety," said he.

"O, no," replied Mrs. Billmer, quite agreeably disposed toward him for the entertainment of his conversation. "The weather was so calm, we were agreed in thinking that nothing could have happened to you."

Elsie was astonished at this falsehood. She had been too deeply absorbed in thoughts of herself to have asked, on her arrival home, whether her brother were there or not; and that Mrs. Billmer as little had thought of him, she was quite sure. Axel saw in her countenance the emotion she felt, but misunderstood it, and, grateful for the anxiety which he believed she had suffered for his sake, he drew her to him, and asked kindly:

"Would n't you like to go with me out upon the water to-day? I mean, would n't it amuse Mrs. Billmer to undertake a sailing excursion? Wind and weather are excellent."

"Yes; why not?" replied Mrs. Billmer. "But the whole forenoon is occupied; eleven o'clock is my bathing hour, and at twelve we must n't neglect the park. But at four it is convenient, and we could be at home again in time for making our toilets before the music begins."

"As you please," replied Axel, with a light bow, and went out.

"Now, how can we gather, in a hurry, a nice little sailing party?" said Mrs. Billmer. "Nollen must go, as a matter of course. May be we can invite Baron S—— and Count P——; but when there are so many gentlemen there ought to be more ladies. Well, I shall do my best."

"Why so many?" asked Elsie, dissatisfied; "it would be so much pleasanter to be alone with Axel."

"Excuse me; not according to my taste," replied Mrs. Billmer, with an air of contempt, and, turning to her French novel, she soon became absorbed in it.

Unusually enough, Mrs. Billmer's plans were not crowned with success. Nollen was the only one whose company she succeeded in obtaining for the boat trip.

When Axel came for them, at four o'clock, he found the faithful satellite ready, with cloaks and shawls upon his arm, rendering himself, as usual, smilingly useful.

The sight was an unwelcome one, and Axel whispered to Else:

"Why did you bring this living clothes-rack along with you?"

"Be thankful to escape with no more of them," answered Elsie, merrily.

As soon as they were seated in the pretty little sailer, it spread its white wings, and shot fleetly through the surging waves.

"How delightful!" exclaimed Elsie, in an ecstasy of enjoyment.

"Yes, it is pleasant," replied Mrs. Billmer. "It is too bad that I could n't succeed in gathering a larger party! One requires lively miscellaneous conversation, in order not to become weary by the monotonous sound of the billows."

"The requisites are so different," remarked Axel, with a sarcastic smile. "For my part, I have not as yet heard enough of the powerful language spoken by the sea, the cliffs, and the wind."

"Such entertainment I envy no one," said Mrs. Billmer. "I should prefer that sea and wind would remain quiet. As to the cliffs, they are utterly monotonous and insignificant."

Axel, who had no desire for continuing conversation, leaned, silent and thoughtful, against the gunwale, and looked out over the swelling waves.

With an impatient motion of her shoulders, Mrs. Billmer turned from him, to bestow her attention upon a more worthy and grateful object, Lieutenant Nollen; and soon they were so deeply engaged in discussing the incidents of the day, in critical remarks upon society in general, and last night's *soirée* in particular, as to forget their silent partners; for not alone

Axel had relapsed in thought—Elsie's childish rapture had given place to seriousness. Powerful thoughts were stirring within her, seizing her soul with wonderfully awakening strength. The fresh bloom vanished from her cheeks; she became so pale as finally to attract the attention and sympathy of Lieutenant Nollen.

"Ah! you are seasick," said he; "we must return immediately. Turn your face toward the wind and try to gape, and perhaps it will pass off. This is a splendid remedy for seasickness."

"I am not sick," said Elsie.

"What ails you?" asked Axel, aroused. "Why are so pale?"

"My soul trembles before the presence of God," replied Elsie. "I have never before had such a sense of him as now."

These words were only for Axel, and spoken in a tone so subdued that only he could hear them; while the rest of the company, believing that Elsie was only a victim to the pangs of seasickness, renewed their merry conversation, leaving her unmolested.

Axel looked at Elsie with a tender, grieved look; and, drawing her nearer to himself, he whispered:

"How can a sense of the presence of God cause my little sister to tremble? Is n't love to

God the sunshine in which she lives and has her being?"

"It has been," replied Elsie, "or—I thought it was; but now my heart is so full of sin that, like Adam after the Fall, I wish to hide myself from the presence of God."

With painful surprise, Axel listened to this confession.

"Poor child!" said he. "I supposed you were so full of faith and love that nothing in the world could disturb your peace with God."

She reclined her head against his arm, and big tears rolled down her cheeks.

"Dear sister," whispered Axel, tenderly, "try to be calm. We can not very well speak with each other here; but, when we are alone, will you open your heart to me, as when we were children, and had all our joy and sorrow in common?"

"Yes, yes! I long to talk to you about myself, and about—you," she added, doubtfully.

Axel made no reply, but appeared to be suffering; and Elsie hoped to succeed in inducing him to break the silence which so long, like a spell, had bound him.

The boat now sped toward the harbor. Mrs. Billmer looked at her watch, satisfied that the excursion had taken up no more of her time, and said:

"Elsie, we have half an hour for making our toilets, and then it will be time to go to the park."

"I shall remain at home," said Elsie.

"Indeed! O, I had forgotten your seasickness. How are you now?" said Mrs. Billmer.

"Thank you, quite well," was the reply; "but I have no desire for going out."

"As you please," said Mrs. Billmer.

"I will come to you when I see Mrs. Billmer leave," whispered Axel, as he helped Elsie from the boat.

After the deliberation and noise inseparable from Mrs. Billmer's toilet-making, quiet again prevailed in the room, and Elsie sat there alone, longing for the appearance of her brother. Herself and sorrow for her sin had given place to thoughts about her brother. No doubt or fear now obstructed her approach to God in childlike faith and hope. The hour of anguish, in which she recently had wished to hide from the eyes of the Holy Almighty Judge, had been struggled through, and again she had found that Father, to whom, in Jesus Christ reconciled, she confided all her cares. "Love banishes fear."

When Axel came, he found her so absorbed

in thought that she did not perceive his presence until she heard him saying, tenderly:

"Little sister, let me hear what it is that makes your heart so heavy."

She raised her head, and turned upon him a look so beaming that he repented his sympathy. What he had believed to be real grief must have been only a fleeting impression, since she now could seem so happy; but suddenly, as a cloud obscures the bright beams of the sun, was her visage now overspread by a look of seriousness.

"It was sin that depressed me," she began. "Alas, Axel, you do n't know how weak and selfish I am. Think, yesterday, when you believed me full of fear and anxiety on your account, I was at a ball, and danced—occupied only with the pleasures of the moment."

"Well," said Axel, "I see no harm in that; my life was in no peril."

"Do n't say so," replied Elsie. "My thoughts would as little have been upon you if you had really been in peril. Besides, I feel now the danger of the life into which I have been drawn, and my own weakness to resist temptation."

And she described her emotions and impressions after her return home, the dream, and the feeling of dissatisfaction that had filled her during the day, which at sight of the sea, the image of infinity, assumed the form and character of deep sorrow for sin.

"But you seemed so happy when I came in and interrupted your thoughts," said Axel.

"Peace came to me during prayer; but I am so weak. Guide me, help me, Axel! that I may not again fall," said Elsie.

"How can the blind lead the blind? Will they not both fall into the ditch?" replied Axel, gloomily. "I am not a Christian more."

To be sure, Elsie paled; but the surprise she manifested was not as great as he had anticipated.

"What, then, are you?" she asked, mildly.

"Nothing," replied Axel. "Do you see, this is just what is the dreadful matter. Whichever way I turn, I find nothing, nothing to lean upon. I can not and will not show you, step by step, the way by which I was led to unbelief and despair. I believed myself struggling for truth and light, and found only void. Do you remember, when we were children, how, one day we were lying underneath the big oak, gazing upward into the air, while I was trying to convey to your mind the first principles of natural philosophy, the laws of gravitation, etc.,

9

we began to imagine how it would seem if earth should suddenly lose its power of attraction and we should fall from it into space, and you became so frightened that, in perfect terror, you embraced me for security? This sense of having lost foothold and fallen off, in a moral sense, I have come to experience bitterly. I believed myself ascending from one degree of light to another. Revelation appeared to me too obscure and narrow, as antiquated prejudice doomed to fall. For a time, this condition of mind was accompanied with feelings of joy and courage. I seemed to myself so strong, so enthusiastic after truth. But I awoke from this dream, and found my doubts to have ripened into despair. You, and the rest at home, saw how changed I was. I tried to hide my condition of mind, and suffer alone; but I could not succeed. How much pain I have caused you all! I, who once had such ardent dreams of becoming a joy to my father and a support to you—you, whom our dying mother confided to my love! I could not conceal my unhappiness; alas! it was stronger than I. The only thing that gives me a little rest is the sea. When I am out upon it, and listen to its deep sighs, I forget myself; I cease to be a creature of thought, and feel myself only an atom in creation."

Axel became silent, and leaned his pale forehead against the table.

Elsie had sat listening, in fear, by word or movement, to disturb him while he was speaking. Now, she took his hand and said:

"Your illustration is clear to me, and was easily comprehended. I could never forget the terror of that moment. But why do n't you carry out the figure?"

"What do you mean?" asked Axel.

"When I threw myself, crying, into your arms, you pacified me with the assurance that we were resting safely upon the rock, and had nothing to fear. Now, I ask you to gaze no longer into space, but look at the Rock of our Foundation. Rest your soul upon the thought that God is love, and you shall not lose foothold in time or eternity."

Axel raised his head, and was startled at sight of the joyful assurance that animated the countenance of his sister.

"Faith only can rest in God," he replied; "but all the faith I have is that of which the apostle speaks when he says: 'Thou believest that there is a God; thou doest well: the devils also believe, and tremble.' My thoughts seek God, but find only dark unrest."

"Your thoughts seek," replied Elsie; "but

how can one find love without seeking with the heart?"

Axel did not answer this question, and Elsie continued;

"But your heart shows more belief than your intellect will acknowledge."

"How so?" asked Axel.

"Do you suffer from unbelief?" asked Elsie.

"Yes," was the reply.

"This suffering is a sense of missing, and, to a certain degree, you must believe in order to miss," said Elsie.

"Who told you that?" asked Axel.

"The truth," said Elsie.

"Well, what is truth?" queried Axel, earnestly; but without the tone of bitter despair with which he had begun his acknowledgment of unbelief.

"God so loved the world that he gave his only-begotten Son, that whosoever believeth in him should not perish, but have eternal life," said Elsie, throwing her arms around her brother's neck.

Axel was moved, although not vanquished, and a solemn silence ensued, which was finally interrupted by the entrance of Fanny, who came to say that Mrs. Billmer had sent her compliments, with the request that they would not wait supper, as she was going to take hers with Mrs. Colonel D——.

"What a fortunate occurrence!" exclaimed Elsie, when Fanny had retired. "So, we can have the whole evening to ourselves. It is really unfriendly of me to feel glad of Mrs. Billmer's absence; but her society would be to me now a genuine nuisance."

"I can excuse the unfriendliness," said Axel, "and hope you will excuse me for feeling the society of Lieutenant Nollen to be the same."

"I am so ungrateful as to share your feeling," replied Elsie; "although I must acknowledge that a more good-natured, accommodating man could not be found upon earth."

Axel seemed unwilling to resume the conversation concerning himself, and Elsie possessed too much tact to be willing to force upon him advice and admonition. She was happy at the warmth with which he had recalled many incidents of childhood. His words breathed love to her, to the home—a sad longing for the peace of childhood. O, would his heart not open to the only true peace? Would he not return a true believer, a soul refined in the fire? O, if she could only speak with Aunt Lena! At thought of Aunt Lena, a favorite song occurred to her, and, going to the piano, she sang, in soft, pure tones, "A Christian's praise for the assurance of being a partaker in the grace of reconciliation."

Axel listened attentively, and the refreshing words of faith fell like a Spring shower upon his soul. Albeit his heart could not join in the glad song of victory, he was touched by the well-known tones, and the feeling of dark despair that usually held sway over him was transformed into one of sad regret.

"Thanks! God bless and keep you!" said he, and, embracing his sister, bade her good-night.

How otherwise seemed Elsie's chamber to her than when she entered it on the previous night! Then its solitude had almost frightened her; now it seemed peaceful and precious.

O, how full and pure was the joy she now felt, compared with the false, fickle pleasure the ball had given her, and which afterward cost her so much unrest and dissatisfaction!

Chapter XII.

TRUTH AND FALSEHOOD.

FANNY sat, sleepy and vexed, waiting for the return of her mistress, whom she thought inexcusably late.

"It's surely that Lieutenant," she muttered; and at that moment her eye fell upon Mrs. Billmer, who was really approaching, leaning upon the arm of Lieutenant Nollen.

The beautiful moonlight had given opportunity for a long promenade after supper. Mrs. Billmer was in exceedingly good spirits. She had amused herself—and was doing so still—by rendering herself fascinating. Her black eyes glittered in the moonlight. Now she was mischievously merry, now shook her dark ringlets with an air of romantic ecstasy. The little Lieutenant was enchanted. At the moment of adieu, he could not forbear carrying her hand to his lips. His homage was received with a smile of half reproof, half encouragement. The warrior's

courage grew. Yet once more he kissed her
hand, and—then once more; but the third
time it was withdrawn as with sudden conster-
nation. The Lieutenant hastened away, and
Fanny opened the door.

Mrs. Billmer pettishly threw aside her hat
and cloak. She was vexed at such "bold impertinence!" "How dared he?" "You gave
him cause," whispered conscience. "That is
not true," answered selfishness; and conscience,
accustomed to bad treatment, was silent.

Fanny, who had seen the kissing, and partly
understood the position, felt induced, both from
duty and desire, to give her lady a scare.

"It is dreadful how much they talk about
you here, madam," she began.

"About my appearance?" asked Mrs. Billmer,
turning to the mirror a self-satisfied smile that
softened her wrath, and added, with a sigh of
compassion: "Poor ones; it is n't to be wondered at."

"O, of course, every body thinks you are perfectly handsome; but that is n't what I meant,"
said the girl.

"Is it my tasty toilet?" asked Mrs. Billmer.

"No; it is about this here Lieutenant that
goes hanging after you, mistress, like a wasp,"
said Fanny.

"Indeed!"

"Yes, the bathing-maids are awful with their talk, and their employers not much better; for a good many girls have told me that they have heard their mistresses speak really naughty things about you," said Fanny.

"Well, what reply do you make to such contemptible scandal?"

Mrs. Billmer had become pale, and her eyes emitted sparks of rage that almost intimidated Fanny from proceeding, all the more as she saw that the truth, misconstrued through exaggeration, which she had uttered, required the addition of an unmixed falsehood; but she quickly composed herself and said:

"I? Well, I said that they ought to be ashamed, I said; and I know, I said, my mistress has got both husband and child in Norrland, said I."

"And you thought thus to protect me from slander?" said Mrs. Billmer, casting a look of scorn at her simple-minded servant, and then relapsing into thought.

Suddenly she lifted her head, with a look of triumph, and said:

"To-morrow I wish you to tell in confidence all whom you meet that Miss Stark is engaged to Lieutenant Nollen."

"Is it possible!" exclaimed Fanny.

"Yes," said Mrs. Billmer. "But, of course, you must n't say that I told you of this, for they desire that the engagement should not be made public here; but you must appear as if you had found it out yourself, and only told of it for the purpose of explaining why he is so much in our company. If you can manage to have this generally circulated within twenty-four hours, you can calculate upon a good reward."

Fanny, who not for a moment doubted her ability to do as required, humbly thanked her mistress.

Mrs. Billmer lay long awake, grieving at the evil-mindedness of the world, that would not allow one the pleasure of a little "innocent flirtation," which appeared to her as allowable as it was indispensable, while spending time at a fashionable watering-place; but, as her own sense of delicacy had sustained no shock, she soon consoled herself by thinking of the artfulness she displayed in arranging for the execution of her plan to make a match between Lieutenant Nollen and Elsie, or, if this did not succeed, in making the world believe they were engaged. With great esteem for her inventiveness, and no remorse for her folly, she finally fell asleep.

With surprise, but satisfaction, Mrs. Billmer

heard next morning, from Elsie, that she designed spending the forenoon with Axel on the water. An opportunity thus early for speaking with Nollen was quite welcome to her. Nor did she have to wait long. His hesitation as he entered, which seemed caused by mixed feelings of shame and admiration, each struggling for supremacy, was extremely ludicrous.

So great was Mrs. Billmer's inclination to laugh that she had great difficulty in assuming womanly dignity, with which it was now necessary to meet him. However, she did manage to control herself, and cast at the awkward Lieutenant a proud look, who, in his confusion, was making convulsive efforts to bite his mustache.

"I am sorry that Miss Stark is not at home," began Mrs. Billmer.

"Who can miss the moon, when the sun is shedding around him its glory?" said the Lieutenant; and, quickened by his eloquence, he ceased biting his mustache.

"Well, now, speak honestly, and confess that little Elsie's person and fortune immediately produced a pleasant impression," said Mrs. Billmer.

"Yes, that is true," said the Lieutenant; "but who can rule his own heart?"

And, as he spoke, he gave Mrs. Billmer a

look containing as much fire as was possible for his little gray eyes; but Mrs. Billmer seemed all unconscious, and continued, in a patronizing, motherly tone:

"As an old friend, I advise you not to let such an opportunity escape. The girl is good, and easily managed. As yet, she has some overstrained ideas of religion; but that is something that soon evaporates. As to her fortune, I need say no more. Think what a future—without debt, and with a handsome yearly income!"

The Lieutenant became thoughtful. Was it not his duty to listen to the voice of reason? He thought of the sacrifice he should make in giving up his liberty, and this little amour, which just now seemed so pleasant. "O, if Mrs. Billmer were a rich widow," he sighed, "how much happier would I then be!" But he resolved to be heroic, and banish all selfish desires, that he might receive with magnanimity what fate now offered him—a fortune and a wife. That Elsie might possibly have right to a higher destiny than the payment of his debts, was a thought that not for a moment occurred to him. After some silence, he gave a deep sigh, and said, "O, well! it is the path of duty, and this I must pursue."

Mrs. Billmer regarded her victory as almost too easily gained. His admiration for her ought to have rendered it to him a matter more difficult to listen to this advice; and, with a look that again threw him into confusion, she said:

"Much joy! but do n't forget an old friend."

Could he be mistaken? Did not her voice tremble, and her little hand, too, as it rested in his? But when he made an appearance of renewing last night's scene, she quickly drew back, and again stood cold and crushing.

With a sigh, and in thoughtful mood, the Lieutenant took leave; but what would have been his thoughts and feelings could he have seen the unrestrained mirth to which Mrs. Billmer abandoned herself when sure that he was out of hearing.

Little did Elsie surmise, as she entered the anteroom, what arrangement had been made for her during her absence. A feeling somewhat disagreeable awoke in Mrs. Billmer as she met the pure, innocent look of Elsie, in which she read unconscious reproof. Had she for a moment thought of Elsie's happiness when laying plans for her future? No; but why should she not be happy with Nollen? He was just as good as any body else; and thus again she silenced conscience.

It seemed to Elsie that Mrs. Billmer wore a look of dissatisfaction; and, always ready to suspect herself of being at fault, she hastened to apologize for her long absence.

"You must have waited for me," said she.

"O, to be sure, I have missed you," replied Mrs. Billmer; "but it has been still worse for Nollen. He seemed very melancholy when he came and found that you were absent."

"Can he seem melancholy?" asked Elsie, merrily. "I have never seen him otherwise than smiling."

"Fie! what a heartless jest!" said Mrs. Billmer. "He surely deserves that you should show more regard for his feelings."

Elsie, who would not hurt a worm, became quite distressed that her words should have seemed heartless, although she could n't quite comprehend the serious manner in which Mrs. Billmer spoke of Nollen's feelings.

"O, I meant nothing so bad," replied Elsie. "Surely, no one is more willing than I to acknowledge his merits."

"Yes, his merits are great. He is the most amiable and upright young man of my acquaintance. The girl whom he chooses for his wife is a fortunate one," said Mrs. Billmer.

Elsie had a great mind to offer some objection, but peace was dear to her and the theme too indifferent; nor was it necessary to say that she thought him insipid and superficial. She had more agreeable subjects for thought — the pleasant hours spent with Axel upon the water, where it had been her privilege to whisper to him words of hope and encouragement, and find him listen to them willingly, although without reply; while he, on the other hand, had told her of the wonders of creation which had their abode in the depths of the sea, and awakened her interest in the infinite variety moving there.

When, in the course of the afternoon, they came upon the park, Mrs. Billmer left Elsie with a group of young girls, while herself went, with much dignity, and took a seat among the elder ladies, a precaution which she was in the habit of taking occasionally, and regarded as a kind of penance. After having listened for a while patiently to Baroness S——, in her descriptions of her sufferings from rheumatic convulsions, and the suggestions of numerous remedies from the other ladies, she had the satisfaction of seeing one of the young ladies approach her mother and exclaim:

"You can't imagine how absent-minded Elsie is! We have been speaking to her about the most interesting things in the world—amusements

that she ought to enjoy, and other things; but
she has appeared as if she hardly heard what
we were saying—so exceedingly indifferent, and
yet so happy! It is certainly true. See! Mrs.
Billmer can not keep her countenance!"

"I am not aware of what you are speaking,"
said the intriguing woman, assuming a look of
bewilderment.

"Elsie's engagement, of course. All the world
is speaking about it," said the young lady.

"Alas! how busy the world is!" said Mrs. Billmer, sighing and pressing the hand of Mrs. G——,
the mamma mentioned, as if imploring sympathy. "To introduce a young girl into society is
a responsible undertaking. I myself need advice
and guidance. My inexperience and natural gayety render me unfit to fulfill my duty toward the
child confided to my care."

Mrs. G—— found Mrs. Billmer so interesting
in her expression of helplessness and self-accu-
sation that she good-naturedly forgot how she
had held the same opinion with Mrs. Billmer
concerning that lady's fitness for the care of a
young girl.

During the evening, the news of Elsie's engagement came from different directions, and
received from Mrs. Billmer more or less cor-
roboration. The more confidence she saw the

rumor attained, the more cautious she seemed.
No one could suspect that she was the person
who had circulated the story, so she concluded
to deny that there was any foundation for it.
Elsie seemed the only one who was unconscious
of what was passing so near her concerning herself; and the tittering insinuations of the young
ladies escaped her comprehension, as did so
much else of their frivolous talk.

10

Chapter XIII.

THE MEETING.

FEW days afterward, Elsie stood in the common "*dolce far niente*" of Marstrand, watching the arrival of a steamer, when an expression of sudden delight escaped her, and she hastened to meet a fine-looking gentleman attired as a traveler.

"Thorsten! Are you here?" she exclaimed. "O, how glad I am to see you!"

Her happy surprise brought to his cheeks a glow, and no wonder that the open, manly countenance was illuminated with a smile as warm if not warmer than that with which the student used to meet his little friend.

"Thank you, Elsie," said he, and caught both her hands. "How changed you are, and yet just like yourself!"

"Where do you come from?" asked Elsie.

"From Stockholm: I brought much love from your father and aunt," he replied. "The home seemed very empty, although as quiet and good as ever. I stayed there a few days; and now have come here to see you and Axel before returning to my business."

"How kind you are! Come with me to Axel," said Elsie; and, utterly unconscious of the looks of curiosity with which she was being regarded, she took Thorsten's arm, and went to seek her brother.

Mrs. Billmer, who was engaged in lively conversation with an acquaintance whom she had discovered upon the steamer, did not notice the meeting; while Nollen, on the contrary, who during the last few days, with commendable zeal, had put himself into his new relationship, seldom departing from Elsie's side, stood looking surprised and flattened. Who could it be that was so heartily welcomed by his betrothed?

When Mrs. Billmer had waved her last adieu, she became accessible to questioners, by whom she was besieged.

"Who was that elegant gentleman whom Elsie was so glad to see?"

"Could he be an elder brother?"

"No; that is impossible."

"Did you see what a handsome smile he had?"

"Yes; and such beautiful teeth."

Lieutenant Nollen became impatient at hear-

ing the encomiums of the young ladies, and
declared that he could n't help envying the
stranger who only needed to show himself in
order to conquer all hearts.

"Well, Lieutenant Nollen, look out for
Elsie," said Hilda G——, roguishly, and the
young ladies tittered in chorus.

Mrs. Billmer's curiosity being raised to the
highest pitch, she hastened home in order to
have it satisfied. There she found Axel, Elsie,
and the unknown, whom Elsie presented as her
foster-brother, Judge Holt.

Thorsten's address and superior bearing produced so favorable an impression upon Mrs.
Billmer that she resolved to bestow upon him
her most winning smiles and attentions, which
would really have been quite too much for
Nollen, but were received by Thorsten with
calm politeness.

She soon succeeded in usurping the lead of
conversation, from which Axel and Elsie were
excluded. Thorsten, however, was sometimes
graciously afforded an opportunity for speaking.
He had a rare gift for description, and his account of a journey abroad, which he had recently made, was highly interesting. Etiquette
required that he should address his words to
Mrs. Billmer; but his look oftener rested upon

Elsie, and she felt that he was speaking to her.
And she thought of when, as a child, she had
sat so many twilight hours upon his knee, listening while he told stories, sometimes so fantastic and fearful as to frighten her and cause
her to hide her face in his breast. How kind
then he used to be, patting her curly head
while he assured her that there were no such
things as wizards and witches, and that there
was nothing in the world that could hurt those
who loved God!

Why were these reminiscences so precious to
her? She knew not, nor did she ask herself.

Thus the evening passed. As Thorsten took
leave, he found opportunity to ask her, unnoticed:

"Where have your thoughts been? You
have seemed so dreamy!"

"I hardly know," answered Elsie, blushing,
while her eye fell. Had she looked up, and
met the glance which, full of tenderness, rested
upon her, she would perhaps have more easily
comprehended the language of her heart.

How she longed for the next day, and an
opportunity to speak alone with Thorsten!
There was so much she wished to confide to
him: her anxieties and hopes concerning Axel,
her own lack of strength to resist the allure-

ments of society. He should hear all, and he would advise, support, and assist her.. She felt secure and happy in the thought of his protection. But, how strange! hour after hour of the next day passed, and no Thorsten appeared. Axel, too, impatiently consulted his watch, wondering if Thorsten would not soon appear, to go with him on a sailing trip, and had afterward gone out to seek him.

Finally, a step was heard in the entrance, the door opened, and—in stepped Lieutenant Nollen. Never before had he seemed to Elsie so utterly disgusting.

"What unexpected fortune I have in finding the ladies alone!" he exclaimed. "How are you? Your absence from the ball last night caused much regret. There was dancing, and an unusually lively time."

"Was it regret at our absence that made the dancing so lively?" asked Mrs. Billmer, smiling.

"Cruel critic, scoffing at my grief!" said the Lieutenant.

Elsie went to the piano, to escape participating in a conversation that seemed to her so nauseous.

"O, yes; let us hear some music," exclaimed the Lieutenant.

Elsie was proficient in music, and now longed

to give expression in its tones to the dim fore-
bodings and emotions that were stirring within
her. She forgot every thing around her. Never
had she performed so before. Her music and
whole person seemed to gleam with inspiration;
and when Nollen came to the piano, and assumed
a position so expressive of admiration and confidence, she was unconscious of his presence
there. Nor did she see the tall, earnest-looking
man, who leaned against the door-frame, contemplating her with a grief so bitter that it
sought to hide itself behind an appearance of
coldness.

Suddenly the spell was broken—her eye met
his. A chill went through her heart. She believed she read in his looks a disapprobation
that bordered upon contempt, and she thought,
with bitter anguish, "He must have heard how
thoughtlessly and frivolously I have acted—that
I have danced!"

The music ceased. Thorsten entered, and
bowed. He had regained his composure, and
spoke, in a calm, fatherly tone, to Elsie, of her
music, her attainment in which astonished him.

"It was too bad that I should come and
interrupt you," said he; "will you not proceed?"

"No; I am unable to do so," she replied,

turning quickly around, as if to arrange her sheets of music.

Mrs. Billmer now tried to draw Thorsten into an extensive conversation upon music, which act soon drove Nollen from the house, while Thorsten had much difficulty in giving due attention to her shallow remarks.

When Mrs. Billmer had exhausted herself, without having succeeded in engaging Thorsten, conversation dragged, and seemed threatened with a breakdown. It was, therefore, a welcome interruption to the hostess, when Fanny entered to say that a box and trunk had been brought from the steamer, and the carriers were waiting for their pay.

"O, my new dress from Ahlberg, and bonnet from Mrs. Sorenson!" exclaimed Mrs. Billmer. "Excuse me, I shall return in a minute;" and, with a sweet smile, she hurried out to take a view of these treasures.

Elsie and Thorsten were alone. Before, she had avoided looking at him; now, she lifted her head, and her little pale countenance was so sad that the ice around his heart melted. All selfish pain disappeared, and, with thought alone for her, he asked:

"Elsie, is what I have heard of you to-day true?"

"Yes," she replied,

"What will uncle and aunt say?" he continued.

"I hope they will forgive me," said Elsie. "I have written a long letter to aunt, telling her all—my repentance, and all about it."

"How?" asked Thorsten. "Do you already repent this step?"

"Yes; can you doubt this?" she asked, and big, bright tears went rolling down her cheeks. "It was very naughty of me to dance; but you must n't for this reason consider me a hardened sinner."

"Because you danced!" exclaimed Thorsten. "Was this all you had to confess?"

"Yes," answered Elsie.

We should conclude, from the lighting up of joy in Thorsten's dark eye, that he seemed not inclined to judge this sin so severely.

"I was already full of worldly thoughts before I danced," continued she; "but dancing just caused me to feel the danger of the life into which I was throwing myself, and I hope that, after this, I shall be more watchful and faithful."

"Forgive me, you dear, innocent child!" cried Thorsten, seizing both Elsie's hands, which he seemed unwilling to let go.

How, for a moment, could he have believed the rumor of her engagement with Nollen? But had he done her an injustice, he had already suffered the punishment for it. He had experienced a bitter pain, that had opened his eyes to the fact that the child whose image he kept among his dearest recollections had gained a new power over his heart, which was not that of recollection, but of hope. He read in her open eye that she was free, and a rapturous joy filled him. She was so young, so tender, that his lips closed again when he opened them to speak his love. An authoress says that the love of a noble man resembles maternal love; and, like a tender mother, Thorsten wished to shield and keep the beloved one from every disturbing impression, shield her from the world, and— from himself.

"Yes; let the young soul develop quietly! I will trust, and wait patiently," he thought, and let go her hands.

A little silence ensued, which, like the sunshine, seemed to disperse all clouds.

"Tell me something about yourself, Thorsten," said Elsie, "about your every-day life at Tanarp, and how you get along with your aged friend."

"Of my daily life, there is n't much to be

said," replied Thorsten. "Fortunately, I have plenty to do, or the emptiness in a home without family life would be still more felt than it now is. In food, drink, and regularity, nothing is wanting; but female society and a Christian atmosphere all the more so."

"That is hard," said Elsie. "So, you and Judge Dangel do not sympathize in what is of the most importance."

"No," said Thorsten. "He is a man of the world, who goes his way with happy ideas of his own perfection. I believe that religion is the only subject that can irritate him. He calls it cant."

"Well, but do n't you often irritate him then?" asked Elsie.

"At first, I tried to lead him to the subject; but his excitement became so great as to make it disagreeable for us both. And I do n't believe that any blessing results from angry dispute," said Thorsten.

"Well, but it is sad for one to have no influence with a person whose daily company he has, and for whom he feels friendship and gratitude," said Elsie.

"Do you believe that words are a Christian's only weapons?" asked Thorsten. "Yet you are right; it is sad to see him so. My hope rests in the future. If ever I am so happy as to have a loving, intelligent wife, it will be her work to soften and warm the old bachelor's heart, and lead him to the Savior. No one could believe more fervently than I do in the blessing of a Christian family life—I, who in your home was first brought to understand what Christianity is, both to this life and the future one."

When Thorsten spoke of his wife, Elsie felt embarrassed and confused; but his last words gave her thoughts a different direction. She sighed, and said:

"Alas! what can home do? Axel says that he is no longer a Christian."

"Is it possible!" exclaimed Thorsten.

"Yes. Speak with him," said Elsie. "He has opened his heart to me; but what can I do? He listens kindly while I am speaking, and I was so foolish as to think that I could draw him back; but I see I can not. He—"

The door opened; and in came Mrs. Billmer, rustling, smiling, beaming.

"Pardon me, good Judge, for being so exceedingly impolite as to remain absent so long; I had to try on my new dress. What do you say to it, little Elsie?" said she, with a look which plainly told that Thorsten was the one expected to reply, and with a compliment. So, seeing that Elsie's thoughts were elsewhere, he hastened to say;

"Charming!"

"Yes, it is quite pretty. And the bonnet; how do you like it?" said Mrs. Billmer, casting a look of sweetness upon her reflection in the looking-glass.

"It is very lovely," said Elsie, who, indeed, was enough a daughter of Eve to understand the thing, and judge with taste.

"Would it be unreasonable to undertake a little walk in the park?" said Mrs. Billmer, desirous of exhibiting her new toilet. "The Judge, of course, will favor us with his company?"

"Yes; with the greatest pleasure," answered Thorsten, in a lively manner, that was quite misunderstood by Mrs. Billmer; for, as Elsie went to her room for her bonnet, she followed her, and whispered:

"Do you know, he was quite charmed when he saw me? He seemed so grave when he came; but now he looks quite lively and cheerful. I have certainly made a conquest there; a fit recompense for the loss of Nollen, whom you have fooled away from me."

Having spoken thus, she hastened back to Thorsten, without perceiving how Elsie col-

ored, and the disagreeable impression her words
had produced, so apparent in the countenance
of the young girl, whose ears had never been
accustomed to unseemly jest.

Chapter XIV.

"BE NOT WISE IN THINE OWN EYES: FEAR THE LORD,
AND DEPART FROM EVIL."

SOME hours later, we find Thorsten and Axel walking slowly along the road that leads from the quay to the powder-magazine, protected on one side by the gray wall of cliffs, on the other threatened by the sea, whose powerful waves occasionally threw surging scum to the feet of the rovers. They seem to be enjoying the grand appearance of the sea, which in turbulent tones is singing its deep, wailing song.

However, the thoughts of Thorsten are more occupied with the storm which he believes raging in the breast of his silent friend than that which was rising upon the ocean. He longed to reach him a helping hand; but feared unbidden to seek Axel's confidence, lest he should awaken the irritable pride that he knew so well of yore. It was, therefore, an unexpected pleasure to him, when Axel suddenly turned toward him with the question:

"Do you believe in the doctrine of reconciliation?"

"Yes," answered Thorsten, firmly. "Are you one of the many unhappy ones who reject the only way to life and blessedness?"

"I do not seek to reject; but I can not understand. I feel myself rejected, lost, and miserable," said Axel.

"It is good for you to have come so far," remarked Thorsten.

"Do you scoff at me?" asked Axel.

"No; God forbid that I should do so," replied Thorsten. "You see your peril, and it surprises me that you have so soon had your eyes opened. An outspoken joy is more common with young heroes of skepticism."

"There was a time," said Axel, "when I felt this joy; but it procured for me no peace. I believed I had found the right way to bliss in the enlightenment of my intellect, and I went quickly forward; but what I sought I never found. So long as I was engaged only in demolishing and rejecting, my courage was firm, and my belief in an ideal beauty that, as I expected, was to spring out from amid the ruins. I was happy, and full of anticipation. All educational bias was thrown off. Christ and Christianity I arraigned in their original beauty at the bar of human reason; but, with horror, soon found that all the Christ that was left me was an empty shell, and I threw away the last splinters of the faith of my childhood. I would not so much as be called a Christian. Philosophy became my only hope; but as yet it has not given me peace, nor has it been any staff to me—and I am so weary, O, so weary! From the depths of my heart, I long to go back to the peace of my childhood."

As Axel spoke, his emaciated features bore the stamp of intense suffering.

"Why, then, do you not obey the voice that calls you back?" asked Thorsten, tenderly.

"There is no retrogression in human development," answered Axel.

"Yes; there you are right," answered Thorsten. "You must experience the new birth."

"How?" asked Axel; "does not your reason rebel against such unnatural teaching?"

"No," replied Thorsten; "but it certainly must rebel against any denial of what I have myself experienced."

"What, then, is the new birth?" asked Axel.

"I can give you no other answer than that which the Master himself gave: 'The wind bloweth where it listeth, and thou hearest the sound thereof, but canst not tell whence it cometh and whither it goeth: so is every one that is born of the Spirit.'"

"O, it is very convenient to come with this obscure oracle," said Axel, impatiently. "Tell me what you have experienced."

"I fear that my experience would give you little satisfaction. It is what every Christian must go through—an experience of sin and grace," replied Thorsten.

"And are you sure of possessing the grace of God?" continued Axel.

"Yes! God is a God of holiness and truth. How could I,-then, doubt his Word?" said Thorsten.

"Elsie, too, speaks of the grace of God with an assurance of faith that sounds to my ear like sweet distant music, the strains of which only serve to render the distance perceptible. I listen willingly to her words; but they only increase the hopelessness I feel afterward," said Axel.

"Dear Axel!" exclaimed Thorsten, "do banish this sickly despair! Humble yourself before the Lord! Lay down your weapons of rebellion, and think not to climb to heaven upon the web of human reason, or that your intellect can throw light upon the Word of God, when, on the contrary, it is the Word of God that must enlighten you. Pray for light; and, even should you have to wait for its bestowment, do not despair! Through prayer you submit your cause into good hands. With all respect for theology and philosophy, I advise you to shut your books and look around in life. To be sure, there is much misery in the world—no one has a better opportunity for seeing this than a lawyer; but, too, there is much to be found of a different character, worthy our attention and interest. Shake off the dust of books, and study man. Perhaps, in doing so, you will more easily understand yourself."

Axel listened attentively. His countenance brightened.

"Thanks for your advice," said he. "My resolve is made. I shall go abroad in the Fall. I think father will be willing."

Thorsten started, and said:

"So soon decided? Then may my advice prove to be as good as it is well-meant! But do not follow it half-way; for then your condition might become all the worse. It is not for the sake of enabling you to forget your disquiet, but for the sake of your health, I recommend you to change air. Peace you will never find among men—only in the Son of God."

"And do you believe that I can find him—I, who have denied him?" said Axel.

"Do you remember how it went with Peter when he denied his Lord? 'Jesus turned and looked upon him,' the Bible says. Don't you think that it is this look of his that awakened unrest in your soul? And after, like Peter, you have wept bitterly, the day, too, will come, when with him you can answer our Savior's question, 'Simon, son of Jonas, lovest thou me?' 'Lord, thou knowest all things. Thou knowest that I love thee.'"

Thorsten spoke with a strength and assurance that seemed prophetic, and his words thrilled the soul of Axel. Elsie had succeeded in awaking a longing within him, but Thorsten yet more. He showed him not only the lost paradise, but also the one regained—a hope for his life. Far away, it lay unattained before him; but it beckoned him forward! He felt like a weary wanderer in the desert, ready to drop from thirst and fatigue, seized by a strong hand that pointed to a gushing fountain. O, how refreshing was this thought, although his parched lips had not as yet tasted "the living water!" He leaned against the wall of the cliff, and threw a long look over the sea—not a wandering and restless one, as when he sought in its hollow roar the resonance of his own pain, but one which seemed to have an aim outside the boundary of material things. Half unconsciously, a sigh escaped him—a sigh that arose upon the wings of prayer.

"You must not think," said Thorsten, "when I ask you to close your books, that I mean the Bible also. No; let this accompany you, and become your light and your staff."

"How shall it become a light to me, when I find it only a dark saying, full of contradictions?" asked Axel.

"Then you have not sought light in it," said Thorsten. "You have read the Bible in the character of a master, and not with the mind of a disciple."

"It can not become clear to me before my intellect has grasped it. If this is what you call reading it in the character of a master, then your assertion is right. I acknowledge no other way to spiritual development than that which is illuminated by my intellect."

The desire for argument had again flamed up in Axel, driving out the better feelings which so recently had stirred in his heart.

"Alas! Axel," said Thorsten, "you speak like one who knows not that there is a Holy Ghost. The preaching of the Cross is, and will ever be, to the Jews a stumbling-block, and to the Greeks foolishness. Human reason can never form any conception of the mystery of the love of God, revealed in Jesus Christ, until the heart, through the operation of the Holy Ghost has experienced its divine power. Then reason, too, will find a firm pillar of support in the simple fact, 'Thus it is written.' Then we receive the Word as the living truth, which, amid the darkness of life and the hour of death, pours upon us its light and consolation."

These words produced upon Axel a deeper impression than he was willing to admit. Yet his desire was for contest, and he was not at loss for a reply; but Thorsten kept him back, and said!

"We will not let our conversation go over to useless dispute. I am determined, if Providence permits, to come to you again in a year from next Fall. Answer me then."

They had left the path, and now met a crowd of promenaders, among whom was Lieutenant Nollen, who deemed it expedient to improve this opportunity for seeking a familiar footing with his future "brother-in-law."

"See 'The Hermit upon John's Shoal,' 'The Viking,' and I do n't know how many romantic names our young ladies give you," said Nollen, scizing Axel's arm, to which manifestation of friendship he not very willingly submitted.

"Judge," he continued, turning to Thorsten, "You can not imagine what coquetry this young gentleman displays. He steps forward as a misanthrope, and has produced an effect that is incredible. When one has black hair, and dark eyes, he can not choose a better *genre*. Too bad, that I am not of that style."

"If Axel is appreciated, it is through his absence. One should try this," said Thorsten.

"Thanks for your advice. It is unselfish," replied Nollen, fancying himself overpowering. He regarded Thorsten as a dangerous rival, who, in a low, intriguing manner sought to rob him of the fortune which he considered already his own.

"If Lieutenant Nollen is so grateful for good advice, I can give more," said Thorsten.

"No, thank you! I need no legal assistance," replied the little man, flaring up, and looking so ludicrous as to draw from even Axel a smile; and, as Nollen felt that Thorsten's calmness was liable to irritate him more should their words go on, with a proud look, and the dignity of a provoked turkey-cock, he bowed, and passed on.

"And he was to become Elsie's husband,"

said Thorsten, gazing smilingly after the ludicrous little figure.

"Who has spoken such nonsense?" asked Axel.

"I have heard it from at least twenty persons," answered Thorsten.

"Are people blind?" said Axel. "Do they not see that he is chained to the wheels of Mrs. Billmer's triumphal chariot?"

"As to his intentions, other people may be more keen-sighted than you are," replied Thorsten; "but they seem to forget that Elsie's consent is requisite."

"He can not be so foolish as to venture to hope."

"Why not?" said Thorsten. "He pursues Elsie like a shadow; and if you had seen how he stood leaning over the piano, when she sat performing there this morning, you would doubt neither his intentions nor anticipations."

"What impertinence!" exclaimed Axel; "but the fault is Mrs. Billmer's. She has encouraged and invited him from the moment we first stepped upon shore here, and, with a punctuality that would do honor to a city messenger, he has gone running around, performing all her errands. It has never occurred to me that he had any time to think of Elsie."

"Then you could n't have given much attention to him."

"No; his presence annoys me. His and Mrs. Billmer's gossip is unendurable."

"So you resigned the pleasure of it to Elsie," said Thorsten.

"You mean that I have acted in a manner miserably selfish; and you are right," said Axel. "But what can I do for Elsie? How rid her of this human wasp?"

"It seems as if you would like to throw him into the water," said Thorsten; "but all I can advise you to do is to give more time and attention to your sister. What Elsie most needs is the presence here of some elderly lady friend when Mrs. Billmer seeks to draw her into pleasures that wound her conscience. I am glad to say that I have an aged female friend here, who will be pleased to take Elsie into her friendship when she becomes acquainted with her. Mrs. Hervig is a lady of uncommon cultivation, and, what is more, a warm Christian. She is a widow, and lives within my jurisdiction, on an estate belonging to herself and two sons. I have received much hospitality at her house, and once had an opportunity to do her a service that gained for me her friendship. She is here in the hope of overcoming the effect of a long and painful

rheumatic fever, by which she was confined to
her bed the greatest part of last Winter. I am
just now thinking of calling upon her, and shall
speak to her of Elsie. Mrs. Hervig is, by her
disease as well as taste, kept from mingling in
the social life here; but Elsie will find a quiet,
pleasant retreat in her society, when she does
not wish to accompany Mrs. Billmer, and can
not accompany you."

"A sick-room would certainly be a sure retreat both from Nollen and Mrs. Billmer; but it
seems to me to be a somewhat dismal one for a
girl of seventeen," said Axel.

"Mrs. Hervig is an invalid, but not sick," replied Thorsten. "I have no intention of shut-
ting Elsie up in a sick-room. Mrs. Hervig loves
flowers and fresh air as much as Elsie herself;
and I shall be much mistaken if a better affin-
ity does not exist between them than between
Elsie and Mrs. Billmer."

"There is no harm in trying," said Axel.
"I comprehend fully what advantage it would
be to Elsie to have good female society. You
deport yourself toward her in a manner more
brotherly than I have done."

"O, do n't say so. I am a great egotist,"
replied Thorsten, and disappeared within the
door of the house occupied by Mrs. Hervig.

Chapter XV.

VANITY.

IN Mrs. Billmer's sleeping apartment, dresses, etc., lay spread over all the chairs and tables, for the sake of reviewal and selection. The tired-out, vexed appearance of Fanny witnessed that the scene had already lasted long, although Mrs. Billmer had not as yet been able to make the all-important decision in what dress she should appear for making her new conquests.

"Elsie! Elsie!" she cried, impatiently; "come here and help me!"

"Here I am," responded Elsie. "What do you wish?"

"Tell me which dress to wear to the *soirée* to-night."

"That is very becoming to you," said Elsie, pointing to an elegant orange-colored one.

"I wore that at the last *soirée!* How can you make such a thoughtless proposal?"

"The light gray barege, then?"

"No, it is not becoming—it is too quiet," said Mrs. Billmer.

"The handsome brown silk, then?"

"It is too dark," replied Mrs. Billmer; "and I am no old woman, although I can not boast of being seventeen."

"You see I am unable to advise," said Elsie, smiling, and was about to return to the inner room, where she had been occupied with copying music.

"How unfriendly you are, to feel so little interest in me," said Mrs. Billmer. "It is almost time to begin dressing; and yet I do n't know what dress I am going to wear. I would like to wear the light green, lustrous gauze, if I liked the trimming; but that would have to be changed, and there is no time."

"O yes, there is," said Elsie, glad of an opportunity for retrieving her character. "You, Fanny, and I will all take hold, if only you know how you will have it."

"Thank you, dear little Elsie," said Mrs. Billmer. "You are very kind. I'll have it trimmed exactly like the dress Countess G—— wore—the light gray silk, you know."

The sound of the door-bell interrupted a detailed description of Countess G——'s dress-trimming; and Fanny, who went to open the door, soon returned with the compliments of Judge Holt, who asked if it was convenient for the ladies to receive him.

"He is very welcome," said Mrs. Billmer, whose ill-humor had quite disappeared at prospect of having the dress righted. "Fanny must sit here and rip, while we take the waist with us to the sitting-room."

Mrs. Billmer threw a hasty glance toward the looking-glass, and met Thorsten with an apology.

"Excuse us, good Judge," said she, "for being a little occupied. We have several little toilet matters to arrange for the evening *soirée*."

"O, are the ladies bound there?" asked Thorsten, giving Elsie a look of surprise.

"I am not," said Elsie, firmly.

"What do you mean, my dear?" asked Mrs. Billmer, a little sharply.

"I mean that I am not going to the *soirée*," said Elsie.

"How capricious! and without letting me know of your decision!"

"Excuse me," said Elsie. "You have not asked me whether I was going; and I had n't as much as thought of there being a *soirée* to-night, until I heard you speak of going, a moment ago."

"O, you are afraid that you can not get ready in time; but any one of your light dresses is suitable, and you need be at no trouble," said Mrs. Billmer.

"I do not lack a dress to go with, but a desire," said Elsie.

"How can you say so?" asked Mrs. Billmer. "Did you not confess to Nollen that you never could have imagined how pleasant it is to dance?"

"I found pleasure for the moment, after first having been drawn into the whirl," said Elsie; "but it would be repulsive to me to go there again."

"Well, but must one persuade you anew every time?" said Mrs. Billmer. "Help me, Judge Holt! Last time, it was Nollen who succeeded in overcoming her scruples."

"Forgive my lack of gallantry; but I can not obey the summons to assist in this case," said Thorsten.

"Is it possible for one who has your culture and intelligence, Judge, to disapprove of dancing?" asked Mrs. Billmer, in surprise.

"I regret to show myself unworthy your flattering opinion, Mrs. Billmer—that is, if you consider a high regard for dancing as necessary to culture and intelligence," said Thorsten.

"O, no fine words! I demand only the acknowledgment that dancing is innocent," said Mrs. Billmer.

"As to this, every one must be his own judge," said Thorsten; "but that all who feel dancing wrong ought to be excused from any persuasion to participate in it, seems to me indisputable."

"But what will the world say, if I go to the *soirée* without Elsie?"

"Do not let any thought about Elsie disturb your pleasure, Mrs. Billmer," said Thorsten. "I have taken the liberty to promise her, on my own risk, for the evening, to Mrs. Hervig, an old friend of mine, who desires to make the acquaintance of my sister."

"Mrs. Hervig!" exclaimed Elsie. "Is it the handsome old lady with silvery hair and friendly eyes, whom I have seen at church, and who interested me so that I could n't rest until I had learned her name?"

"Yes, just the same," said Thorsten. "When I spoke of you, she said: 'Is it that blonde'—I must skip the adjectives—'whom I have so often seen and wished to know?'"

"O, how pleasant!" exclaimed Elsie.

"Then may I take you to her?" asked Thorsten.

"Yes, indeed," replied Elsie.

"Shall you, too, spend the evening there, Judge?" asked Mrs. Billmer.

"No," said Thorsten. "If I may first take Elsie to Mrs. Hervig, I will hope afterward for the honor of accompanying Mrs. Billmer to the hall."

"Well, this is dividing one's attention as befits a true cavalier," said Mrs. Billmer, feeling sure that the greater share was meant for herself, and not suspecting that care for Elsie only could induce Thorsten to forego his desire to spend the evening with her and Mrs. Hervig.

Was Elsie as satisfied with the division of attention? We believe not. She had thought what a congenially minded trio they would form—Mrs. Hervig, Thorsten, and herself—and how much more enjoyment she should have of Thorsten's company with Mrs. Hervig than ever it were possible to have in the company of Mrs. Billmer, who possessed an uncommon tact for usurping the lead of conversation and occupying the attention of surrounders, although without always interesting them. Now Elsie saw her good opportunity lost, and why? Because the same Thorsten who had judged her so severely for dancing now himself wished to attend a ball. No wonder that his conduct seemed to her strikingly inconsistent. With many, it would have been enough to awaken jealousy, distrust, and misunderstanding, the elements which, fitly compounded, form the exciting interest of a novel, and, alas! do in reality embitter many a life.

But Elsie was no heroine of romance, with the power to render life miserable both to herself and others. She looked up to Thorsten, like a child who wonders if it may ask, "Why?" and the look of inquiry did not remain unanswered. The words, "When may I come for you?" were only an insignificant question, and Mrs. Billmer heard them; but she saw not the look accompanying them—that was for Elsie only. Could she fully comprehend its language? Perhaps not. Was not the love they spoke at once so deep and pure as to lead her, in trembling yet indescribable joy, to suspect the existence of a new world, without being able to make to herself any clear idea of its treasures?

"At seven o'clock, I shall be ready," said Mrs. Billmer; "and I think Elsie can be so at half-past six. Half an hour, I suppose, is sufficient for Elsie and Mrs. Hervig?"

"Half an hour sufficient?" thought Thorsten, with a sigh. The ungrateful man, who just now had lived through a half-minute full of the richest joy, was already murmuring at the shortness of time; but, with commendable self-control, he bowed acquiescingly, and took leave.

It was a matter more difficult now for Elsie to understand and perform immediately Mrs. Billmer's directions about the dress; but, fortunately, Mrs. Billmer's thoughts were too much occupied with the all-important work to allow any observation of aught so insignificant as the workings of a human heart.

The reader may accuse Thorsten of wavering in his praiseworthy resolve to keep silent and wait patiently. However, he did not escape without self-reproach. To be sure, he had said nothing; but he would not undertake self-defense, when tried by his own conscience. He had manifested his feelings; and could he possibly doubt the sweet hope that smiled upon him in the look he so recently met? Only a question, and she would have been bound to him for life. She would not have hesitated to give the sacred promise of sharing with him earth's joys and sorrows; but this must not be—as yet; so, with quick steps, he walked around to pass off the time until the hour when he should take Elsie to Mrs. Hervig.

Chapter XVI.

A MATERNAL HEART.

"THE Judge will be here now presently," said Mrs. Billmer, as the clock struck half-past six. "What would he say, if he knew that I had only begun dressing? But the dress is completed; so you can go, Elsie, and prepare him not to expect me ready before an hour from now."

Mrs. Billmer was not mistaken in supposing that Thorsten would be punctual. He was there, and Elsie was soon ready to go with him to Mrs. Hervig.

"Is Mrs. Billmer ready too?" asked Thorsten.

"No," said Elsie; "she asked me to tell you that she can not get ready as soon as she expected. You need n't go for her before half-past seven."

"Need n't!" repeated Thorsten; "do you think that I am impatient for the pleasure of accompanying Mrs. Billmer to the ball?"

"Yes," answered Elsie; "I ought to think
so, since you could judge me so severely."

"Have I judged you severely?" asked
Thorsten.

"To be sure you have," replied Elsie; "you
were so dreadfully grave, and questioned my
repentance, when you spoke to me about dancing; but you asked my pardon — so there is
nothing to be done about it. Perhaps you, too,
intend to dance?" she added, roguishly.

"Yes; if Nollen persuades me," answered
Thorsten.

"Pshaw! How ugly you are!"

"O, no," exclaimed Thorsten. "You ought
rather to say pretty things about me for so
dexterously delivering you from going to the
soirée with Mrs. Billmer, and, too, for preparing
you a place of refuge, where you can hide if the
world, represented in Mrs. Billmer, seeks again
to entice you to do what your conscience disapproves. I give you, in Mrs. Helvig, a trust-
worthy friend."

"Thank you, Thorsten," said Elsie. "You
must have seen how much need I have of help.
Mrs. Billmer says that I never have thought for
myself, and perhaps she is right; for it often
seems to me as if my efforts were like those of
young swallows learning to fly. I have wings,

knowledge and faith, but they seem all too weak. I flutter and flutter; but that is all I can do."

"When Axel speaks about you, it is not thus," said Thorsten. "He envies the strength of your faith."

"O, compared with him, I am quite happy," said Elsie. "I can pray, and in prayer forget all grief and disquiet; but then again come thousands of little temptations and sins, and draw me downward. Then it is I feel that my wings are too weak."

"Yet they carry you," said Thorsten. "Fear not, dear little bird, that He shall leave you— he, without whose will not a sparrow falls to the ground. Be cheerful, and you will certainly see he lets the wings grow!"

"Yes; I believe so," said Elsie, hopefully. "In all my frailty, my heart turns longingly toward what is great and good in life. I would like to be rid of any necessity of seeing what is low and miserable in the world, and cling only to the fact that God is love."

"You desire, then, full blessing while here; but you can not expect in time what is promised for eternity," said Thorsten. "Kjerkegaard says that a Christian life resembles a ship under full sail. When one sees the filling sails, we imagine that the wind moves the ship easily over the swelling waves; but, at the same time, the keel is plowing its furrow in the deep. But here we are, at the end of our walk."

Elsie was disagreeably surprised at the interruption, and felt unprepared for the presentation; but the straightforward manner in which Thorsten, with a significant smile, led her to Mrs. Hervig and said, "Here she is," and the heartiness with which Mrs. Hervig embraced her, caused her soon to feel at home.

"Welcome, dear child," said Mrs. Hervig, giving a searching look into Elsie's eyes. "You were very kind, to give an old lady this pleasure."

"Do n't say so, Mrs. Hervig. I am the one to feel grateful for being allowed to come," said Elsie, in consciousness of having thought mostly upon herself, when with so much pleasure she acquiesced in the arrangement for making this visit.

"I know that we have great interests in common," said Mrs. Hervig, "the same faith and same hope, and even an earthly friend who is dear to us both;" and, with a friendly nod to Thorsten, she added: "Do not seem so uneasy, Judge; take a seat, and let us have a cozy time together."

"I regret that I must decline the enticing invitation," said Thorsten. "My time is promised in a different direction."

"What!" said Mrs. Hervig. "Here Lady Justitia has no claim upon her servants?"

"No," said Thorsten; "but another lady has. I promised to accompany Mrs. Billmer to the *soirée*."

For a moment, Mrs. Hervig gave Thorsten a look of surprise, but, quickly comprehending the position, she nodded approvingly.

"Well, then," she added, "much pleasure; we shall have to be contented without you.

"Wish me, rather, much patience," replied Thorsten, with a smile. "I dislike such a place; and how people with free will and sound reason can, in Summer particularly, spend time so foolishly, is to me quite incomprehensible."

"But why do you submit to such suffering?" said Elsie, who could not see what necessity there was for the offer.

"I have no thought of making myself a martyr," said Thorsten. "When Mrs. Billmer enters the hall, she will be so surrounded that I can retire without being missed, and go out into the park, where I suppose I shall find some reasonable being to talk with. Perhaps I can induce Axel to keep me company."

"I do n't believe you can; he avoids the park," said Elsie.

"Yes; but he has resolved to become more social," remarked Thorsten. "I have given him several matters for thought, that I hope will do him good. Among other things, I have awakened a desire for undertaking a journey abroad, and he will probably leave in the Fall."

"Do you think this will be good for him?" asked Elsie. "How can he, under the constantly changing impressions of a journey, find the light and peace which he so much needs?"

"He must tear away from his melancholy," said Thorsten. "He needs strengthening, mentally and physically, in order not to be consumed by it. Speak with Mrs. Hervig about him. Good-bye!"

Elsie followed Thorsten's advice. She treated Mrs. Hervig with all the confidence due a long-tried friend, and received in return many words of encouragement and good counsel.

From grave topics, conversation turned upon Thorsten.

Mrs. Hervig spoke of him with the warmest kindness and highest praise, and seemed to see with pleasure the interest with which her young visitor listened to her words.

"May God reward him!" she continued.

"He is indeed the protector of the widow and fatherless; this I and many others have experienced."

Elsie's eyes asked for more; however, her lips did not frame an interrogation. Mrs. Hervig understood her, and said, smiling sadly:

"It would be wrong to leave these words without more closely defining them; but, in doing so, I must awaken many sorrowful memories. Yet they are connected with so much experience of grace· that I can look back upon them without bitterness.

"I had been a widow one year when Judge Holt came to our vicinity. My grief at the loss of a dear, noble husband was like that of a heathen. Grief, which ought to have brought me nearer my Savior, showed me that my faith was weak and tottering. It could not carry the cross that had been laid upon me. I abandoned myself to the selfish pain which, like a heavy mist, obscured life to me and those around me.

"My sons, who mourned as youth mourn, when the first pain was transformed into sad remembrance, sought with love and attention to encourage me; but I repulsed them, wounded by the light way in which I thought they carried the loss of such a father.

"My eldest son assumed the management

of the estate, in which he already for some years had assisted; while my youngest son, a happy, uncorrupted youth, who had recently finished his military examination, concluded to study agriculture also, and help his brother. To live for these two dear boys was the work the Lord had given me; but I comprehended not its importance, until with horror I found that my selfish indifference had brought us to the border of destruction."

A deep sigh manifested the bitterness of the recollection, yet she went on:

"My home was gloomy and empty. To be sure, the Word of God was read, according to old custom; but the hours of devotion were to me painful reminders that the voice which formerly presided was now silent forever. I thought only of him, and shut my heart against the comfort offered in the Blessed Word. When my eldest son took his father's place, and with manly emotion read the Word, he seemed to me like a usurper; and when, after he had finished reading the prayer, he came to me, asking in a tender tone if I was pleased with him, I only turned my head away and wept. He did not ask me again; yet his eye evidently sought some look of encouragement, which I never could bestow, and he retired from the effort. A cold indifference took possession of his heart, and filled with poison the entire household. I could but perceive the change, and suffered therefrom; yet I did so without acknowledging that myself was the cause.

"I have already spoken of a peril that threatened us. My youngest son was a proficient in music; but, as he could never now open the piano without driving me from the room, he soon began to seek friends and amusement outside his cheerless home. His visits to town became more and more frequent, and, from amusements comparatively innocent, he was gradually led into such as even the world disapproves.

"From the bowl to the gambling-table the road was not long. The elder brother advised the younger, who became irritated. Words arose between them, and the result was that Theodore, the erring one, forsook his home.

"Now came a time of great sorrow, just the point at which we formed the acquaintance of Judge Holt. My eldest son, Henrik, conceived an immediate friendship for him, and the warm, living Christianity of Judge Holt's life had its genial influence upon the spiritual life of Henrik. My poor Theodore had been sucked deeper and deeper down the vortex into which he had been drawn. He incurred a debt in gaming, which

soon arose to a height that aroused his dread.
But it was not the feeling of a true penitent by
which he was now seized. No! it was horror,
contempt for himself, fright for the future—in a
word, dark and paralyzing despair; so that he
finally hid himself from his new friends also.

"Through what the world calls an accident,
but I call God's providence, Judge Holt was led
to overhear a heartless conversation between
certain reckless persons, in which wonder was
expressed at Theodore's non-appearance, and
the supposition rudely made that he had concluded to hang himself.

"'O, then,' said one of the party, in response to this, 'he will have no fear that, after
clearing out his pockets as you did last Sunday,
you will be after his clothes also; for I doubt
whether he has any thing else left.'

"Holt suspected that there lay underneath
this a fearful truth; and, although having little
acquaintance with Theodore, he resolved to
make immediate search for him. He found his
quarters, but the door was locked. Finally, he
succeeded in finding a woman, whom he asked
for Lieutenant Hervig; but at first she refused
to admit him. 'The Lieutenant had perem.pto-
rily commanded her to admit no one,' she said;
but when Holt assured her that it was of the

greatest importance that he should speak with Theodore, that he did n't belong to the class of gentlemen who were in the habit of coming there, she not only opened the door, but her heart also, telling him her anxieties about the Lieutenant, who, she said, had behaved in such a strange manner lately as to give her alarm.

"Judge Holt had no patience to listen longer, but bade her hasten to open the door. His suspicion had not been misplaced. A single glance was sufficient to show how irreparable might have been the loss of a few moments. He found Theodore, pale and emaciated from mental suffering and sleeplessness, writing with feverish rapidity, while at his side, upon the table, lay a loaded pistol. The door had been opened so cautiously as not to attract his attention; but at the sound of footsteps he started, and exclaimed:

"'Who dares to intrude?'

"'A friend,' said Holt, and laid his hand gently upon Theodore's arm.

"'A friend! Yes; I have many such,' said Theodore, with cutting bitterness, 'and that is just the reason why I have no time to spare.'

"I can not give the conversation that ensued; but sure it is that what Judge Holt then said and did will never be forgotten. Theodore acknowledged to him the whole round of his errors, his despair, and resolution to shorten his life. The letter that he was writing as the Judge entered was for me, he said, and to be his last work before the committal of the deed that would fix his doom."

Mrs. Hervig shuddered at the revolting recollection, and it was some time before she could proceed.

"The Judge must have gained admittance to Theodore's confidence; for he showed him a list of his debts, which he supposed must drive me from my home; for our fortune and only income consisted in the property we held mutually. Inexperienced as he was, and unaccustomed to business, his fears had much exaggerated his real condition. Judge Holt succeeded in convincing Theodore of this, and remained with him several hours, until his excitement was over; when, persuading him to take food, from which he had abstained for two days, and afterward to go to bed, Holt left, promising to come for him in the morning, and take him home.

"What a meeting! What a mixture of joy, sorrow, repentance, dread, gratitude, and hope! My eyes were opened; I saw my own work. The mutual weakness and repentance of his mother and brother seemed to make us more dear to Henrik, whose character showed itself from the most amiable side. Sure it is that this period forms a new era in our home, one in which, although it has had great difficulties and struggles, has had also its rich experiences of God's grace and love. Next God, our gratitude for all our happiness is due Judge Holt."

Elsie was deeply affected, while Mrs. Helvig reclined wearily upon the sofa, closing her eyes; and Elsie ventured not to interrupt the silence until again she opened them, when she reverently carried her hand to her lips, and whispered:

"Thank you!"

Mrs. Hervig drew Elsie lovingly toward her, and said:

"I have opened my heart to you; but I should be a prattlesome old woman if it were my habit to do thus with strangers. But little Elsie, if I may call you so, is no stranger to me. I hope we shall learn to love each other sincerely."

Elsie responded pleasantly, and the evening sped on at such a rate that she was quite surprised when the time came to go home.

Chapter XVII.

DESIGNS AND DELIBERATIONS.

S Mrs. Billmer sat yawning, the next day, over a French novel, and reposing after the last night's exhaustion, Elsie was diligently sewing, thus showing that her object was to use, and not spend time.

After a while, Mrs. Billmer suddenly threw her book aside, and exclaimed:

"I have had a brilliant idea, to which even you, little Puritan, can not deny approval! I have decided to give a *fête champêtre*—a dinner on the green—in some nook among the cliffs. We are going out on a Viking expedition. Pallin, with his serving spirits, must take care of the provisions; and our only care will be to render ourselves agreeable and entertaining. Well, do you see any aunt, with glittering sword, turning to prevent your entrance to this paradise?"

Although this effort at jest was offensive to Elsie, she was pleased at the arrangement. It

promised real pleasure. She was sure of finding
Thorsten's name at the head of the invitation
list, as at present he possessed the transient fortune of Mrs. Billmer's particular favor. Nollen's
presence, pursuing her with his flat attentions,
was a necessary evil, which she was prepared to
endure with patience.

"Yes, it is unquestionably a good plan, if
the company is not too large," said Elsie.

"Well," replied Mrs. Billmer, "I should
judge that about twelve persons would be a
suitable number for such a little picnic. I, you
and your brother, Judge Holt, Nollen, Baroness
S—— with daughter and son (you know the
young Baron S—— who taught you to dance
française), and Mrs. Colonel D——. There
we have five ladies and four gentlemen, consequently three vacancies to fill. Two more
young gentlemen would n't be out of place.
Yes, this will be delightful! I shall get the
thing going immediately. To-morrow fits excel-
lently, if the weather permits. Will you go
with me to the park?"

"Thank you, but I have no time," said Elsie.

"Time? O, how absurd! What necessary
work are you engaged in, if I may ask? Cot-
ton goods, I see."

"I am making a dress for a poor little girl."

"O, how lovely!" cried Mrs. Billmer, scornfully. "Can we not even here be free from beggars? I see enough of dirty, hungry, ragged youngsters at home. I really wish here to escape all reminders of such annoyances; and I demand that you draw none of the rabble here. It is enough to be obliged to meet such objects upon the street, and hear their whinings there."

"If you had seen the bright-eyed, neat little girl for whom I am making this, you would have found the sight far from disagreeable," said Elsie; "besides, she is not under my protection. It was Mrs. Hervig who gave her the dress, and I offered to sew it; for Mrs. Hervig can not, on account of the rheumatism in her hands."

"O, yes, that's all very fine. Keep at the sewing, in the hope of gaining admiration," said Mrs. Billmer; and her cold, scornful words could not be otherwise than as a drop of bitterness upon the innocent pleasure which Elsie found in her little work; but, when she was alone, every unpleasant impression soon disappeared, and her thoughts again, while plying her needle, were full of cheer.

After the lapse of a couple of hours, Mrs. Billmer returned, beaming with good humor, accompanied by Thorsten and Nollen. She had hardly entered before she called out to Elsie:

"Hear, my little friend! Now you will have a splendid chance for showing the goodness of your heart! The directors of the public amusements ask you to step forward as one of the ministers of Mercy. I am to represent Mercy. The costumes are to be ordered from Gothenburg, and the whole promises to be *charmant*."

"What is the meaning of this?" asked Elsie, looking in surprise from Mrs. Billmer to Thorsten.

But a half-suppressed, satirical smile was all she obtained from the latter, and Mrs. Billmer continued:

"The meaning is that I, Mercy, sit upon a throne, and, through my ministering spirits, distribute gifts to the poverty and want that lift their hands imploringly around. Acknowledge, Judge Holt, that the idea is a beautiful and touching one! I predict that it will draw tears into many eyes."

"It will certainly be enough to weep at," said Thorsten, gravely. "It is a cutting satire upon the charity of our day."

"How?" asked Mrs. Billmer, as surprised as Elsie recently had been.

"It is dramatic nonsense," continued Thorsten; "a trifling with life's bitterest realities; a folly as hurtful to the giver as to the receiver."

"Are you not too severe?" asked Elsie, modestly venturing a remark.

"I do not deny that such undertakings may contain much good-will, and zeal even; but it is a wrong way for dispensing charity. Beggary has become an enervating and demoralizing disease. The healing strength, which, rightly used, would elevate and invigorate society, is not only wasted, but brings forth curse instead of blessing."

"To say that society is diseased is quite common," said Nollen; "but tell me, where is the remedy?"

"In a living, healthful Christianity, a better acquaintance with both the spirit and letter of the Bible. This is what is needed by both poor and rich," replied Thorsten.

"O, is nothing more than Christianity required?" said Mrs. Billmer, trying to turn off the serious tone of the conversation by a jest. "Then the want may soon be supplied; for at present we are almost deluged by Christianity."

"It is to be regretted that there are all too many who allow themselves to be deluged rather than penetrated by Christianity," said Thorsten, who was so engrossed in his subject as to seem not likely soon to leave it; and Mrs. Billmer deemed it necessary to interrupt him.

"Well, my good Judge," said she, "this is certainly true and excellent altogether, I will not dispute; but let us return now to the principal question."

"To the costumes?" asked Thorsten.

Mrs. Billmer found Thorsten's smile very annoying, as she replied:

"No; the costumes are already ordered. I mean my question whether Elsie will give her service to Mercy."

"I will gladly serve both you and mercy, but not in a *tableau vivant*," replied Elsie, feeling that she had a protector at her side.

"Again a refusal?" said Mrs. Billmer. "But consider how ungrateful this is toward the directors, who showed me the courtesy to think of you; and the poor, too, who have the income from the sale of tickets. How can you be so hard-hearted? To be sure, there will be labor and fatigue in it; but what will not one do for his suffering neighbor?"

Elsie could not be moved; and, after all, Mrs. Billmer took her refusal quietly, remembering how much more assistance she was likely to have from Elsie than were she to have a costume of her own to look after. She liked, too, that her servants should be her inferiors in beauty, which would not have been the case with Elsie.

After an extensive detail of what was to be done in order that the affair should be a brilliant thing for the poor, Mrs. Billmer said:

"O, Elsie! I forgot to tell you that our plan for to-morrow seems likely to meet with excellent success. I have got 'Yes' wherever I have turned."

"The person who was so fortunate!" whispered Nollen, with a languishing look, to Elsie.

"Are you not invited, sir?" she asked.

"O, yes!" he replied; "but I meant Mrs. Billmer was fortunate to have obtained a 'Yes.'"

He sighed, and found even himself that he was flat; and Elsie turned away without answering.

"Shall we gather at two o'clock?" asked Thorsten.

"Yes, and in Paradise," answered Mrs. Billmer. "From there we shall start."

"To land where?" asked Thorsten.

"It depends upon circumstances," replied Mrs. Billmer. "We shall take our kitchen with us, so can leave it with wind and weather to decide our fate."

Chapter XVIII.

"BOAST NOT OF THE DAY BEFORE THE EVENING."

WIND and weather carried Mrs. Billmer and her guests to an enchanting little valley among the cliffs, where proud oaks, fragrant capritolium, pretty entanglements of woodbine, and many other children of the "green-locked Hertha," were shielded from the rough sea winds. The sky was cloudless, the air salubrious, the dinner faultless, and the solemn gray cliffs resounded with the merriment of human voices. The sun began to lower, and the two elder ladies suggested the propriety of starting homeward; but the lively hostess asserted that it was much too early.

"We must first look around," said she. "Here we have been for several hours in the same place. Do any wish to go with me among the mountains on an exploring tour?"

"I do! I do!" shouted the young people;

and it was resolved that half an hour should be
spent thus in roving about, after which the
whole party should meet at the boats.

Mrs. Billmer thought it too prosy to walk
along the paths; so she ran ahead, among
bushes and rocks, declaring that her companions
must follow her, like faithful subjects.

"Yes; to death!" answered Nollen.

"To the abyss; but no farther," said Baron
S——, laughing, as he overtook Mrs. Billmer,
who had stopped at the edge of a wide, deep
cleft in the mountain.

"No farther than the abyss, then," said Mrs.
Billmer, laughing.

"No, gracious lady," replied the Baron; "it
is contrary to my principles to promise more
than I can perform."

"Then I suppose I must bid you to remain
here; for over the gulf it seems impossible to
pass, and into it I think no one has the desire
to follow me; although, if this should be one of
the porches of hell, the entrance is not wanting
in pictorial beauty," said Mrs. Billmer.

Nollen laughed uproariously at this superb
jest. Baron S—— smiled. Miss S—— looked
abashed, and as if uncertain whether one *comme
il faut* should listen to an expression so frivolous. Elsie turned away with dissatisfaction;

and Thorsten was grave, but said nothing. As Mrs. Billmer received no reply, she said, gayly:

"One trophy, at least, I shall carry with me, even though His Subterranean Majesty himself should oppose. This handsome branch of caprifolium shall be mine."

So saying, she bent quickly forward over the steep precipice to pluck it. Her foot slipped, a shriek was heard—and Mrs. Billmer had disappeared.

For the moment, all were stupefied. Not a sound, not a groan, was heard. The silence was awful. Who should first venture a glance downward, to see the recently arrogant, trifling being transformed into a mangled corpse?

Thorsten was the first to look over, but the sight that met him was not so horrifying as he had expected.

"Hush!" he whispered; "there is a possibility of saving her. She is not dead; but, if she should revive from the swoon she is in, a slight motion is enough to hurl her irretrievably down the abyss."

Now the rest of the party approached cautiously and gazed down, where they saw Mrs. Billmer entangled in some blackberry-bushes that grew upon a projection of the mountain wall. Below this little projection the walls were perpendicular, and nothing was to be seen but the dark, damp chasm, which now seemed ready to swallow her; but above the bushes were smaller projections, which rendered a descent to her possible, although extremely perilous. Thorsten conceived the possibility of this; but, fearing too much excitement among the spectators, he whispered to the trembling young ladies:

"Hurry to the boat and procure assistance— but quietly."

His plan was conveyed to the rest more by signs than by words. Few and slippery were the footholds; but, steadily and slowly, he began to descend, fearful of making the slightest noise that might arouse Mrs. Billmer. He succeeded in reaching the bush that held the still unconscious woman, found a sure foothold, and then stooped down to lift her. She opened her eyes and glared wildly around; then uttered a piercing shriek, and clung to Thorsten with such convulsive strength that he turned pale, and was near slipping.

"Save me! save me!" she cried, in a tone of indescribable horror.

"Yes; with God's help," said Thorsten. "Only keep still, and let go my right arm. I can not move without the free use of it."

Mrs. Billmer obeyed mechanically, and shut

her eyes. The ascent was much more difficult than the descent had been; for, besides the burden of Mrs. Billmer's person, her fluttering clothes were constantly catching upon sharp stones and bushes. Finally, they had come so far up that Axel, by lying prostrate, could reach Mrs. Billmer, With more haste than care, he assisted Thorsten to get her up and place her upon the spot where before she had stood, so full of gayety.

"Thank God!" she muttered. "How dreadful it would have been to die! Die! die! must I die?"

Seized by wild fright, she shrieked again, and tried to raise herself.

"I fall! fall! Help! help!" she cried; and again fainted, ·falling toward Nollen, who hastened to support her.

"Delirium," said Nollen, looking alarmed, and pointing to his forehead.

"Possibly; but not there," answered Baron S——, pointing at Mrs. Billmer's head; "only a quite natural shaking up of the nerves. We must manage to get her away from here as quickly as possible."

Meanwhile, Elsie and Miss S—— came running toward them, accompanied by the boat's crew, who were provided with ropes, and such

other means of rescue as were available. Axel
hastened to meet them, with the glad tidings
that Mrs. Billmer was saved.

"How? By whom?"

"There is the hero," said Axel, pointing to
Thorsten, who stood, grave and pale, leaning
against the wall of the cliff.

Elsie flew toward him, forgetting Mrs. Billmer and all else for the peril to which he had
been exposed, and the heroic courage he had
manifested.

"O Thorsten, you have risked your life!"
said she. "How could you? What if you—"
Her quivering lips refused to speak the mournful possibility.

"If I were dead, you mean," said Thorsten,
looking with tenderness into her tearful eyes.
"Yes; I am grateful that I was not called by
sudden death into eternity, although my hope
and faith in Him who has taken away the sting
of death did not seem to falter; but, when I
held in my arms a being so apparently in danger.
not only of death, but the judgment, such a
stranger to the only light that can disperse the
darkness of death, my feelings were wonderfully
solemn. May this deliverance from death be to
her the means of an awakening to life!"

Elsie, from her heart, responded to this wish.

Both now approached the group surrounding Mrs. Billmer, and saw her come again to consciousness, but without power as yet to move or speak. She was carried to the boat, where a bed of cloaks and shawls had been prepared for her. After moaning awhile, she could finally articulate:

"I am crushed! My head! my head! my arms! my back! O, it is dreadful! I shall certainly be a cripple for life!" And she moved backward and forth, in a manner which evinced more strength and vigor of limbs than patience.

"Dear Mrs. Billmer," said Baroness S——, patting her kindly, "do not be so anxious. We will hope for the best."

"Anxious!" repeated Mrs. Billmer. "How could I be otherwise, with such indescribable pain, and the prospect of perhaps being disfigured forever? O, why should I return to such a life? It would have been better to have died down there."

"Hush!" whispered Elsie, earnestly, almost sternly; "you do n't know what you are saying. Think of what it is to die, and thank God that you live."

Now Mrs. Billmer fell into a kind of spasmodic hysterics that frightened the whole company, and not least among them the poor Elsie,

who felt herself the cause of this new increase
of suffering.

However, after a while her sobs were succeeded by an unquiet sleep, interrupted by
violent starts and cries: "I fall!" or, "Help!
help!"

"On arriving at Marstrand, the guests accompanied the unfortunate hostess home; after
which they took leave, to tell, each in his own
direction, as soon as possible, the sad, remarkable incident of the afternoon; but, above all,
his own feelings and impressions, and the con-
spicuous part each one had acted.

However, in justice to Nollen, the reader
must be informed that he relinquished the
pleasure of first publishing the calamity, and
was really the one to bring the doctor, who,
after a careful examination, found that Mrs.
Billmer was suffering from some insignificant
contusions, and a severe shock of her nervous
system, which needed perfect quiet during some
days, perhaps weeks.

However comforting this assurance was, and
suited to the calling forth of gratitude, it only
awakened in Mrs. Billmer a feeling of dissatisfaction at being considered less ill than she believed she really was.

After wishing his patient a quiet night, the

doctor left the room; and Elsie, who, as the door opened, saw Thorsten, Axel, and Nollen waiting in the outer room to hear the result of, the doctor's examination, only nodded them a good-night, leaving them to obtain their information concerning Mrs. Billmer from the doctor. She would not for a moment leave the sufferer.

"Where is Fanny?" asked Mrs. Billmer.

"Gone for ice. May I help you?" asked Elsie.

"Light the lamp. I do n't like darkness; it reminds me of the black chasm. O Elsie, it is so horrifying! Come nearer. Let me hold your hands. I can 't help thinking how dreadful it would be if I were now lying down there. O, it seems so dark and damp when—think, how much darker it must be there now, with night hanging over it, and so desolate! No human voice—only the distant moaning and roaring of the sea. You can not imagine how it pains me to think how this abyss, that sought to swallow me, is yet holding open its fearful gap, as if calling, in scorn, 'I am waiting for you! you shall not escape me.' O, that I could crush the cliffs, or cause this fearful chasm to be filled!" and, letting go Elsie's hand, she wrung her own, in anguish.

"You misunderstand your fears, I believe,"

said Elsie, making an effort to be calm. "It is not the mountain chasm that causes it. It is the abyss of death and sin that arouses your horror. But do not allow this feeling to drive you to despair; for you know that these powers are vanquished for you, if only your heart is open to the victor."

"Are you not afraid to die, then?" asked Mrs. Billmer, in surprise.

"I hope that I am not," replied Elsie, "although life seems so sweet to me that my nature shrinks from the thought of death; but I know that God's love will guide me through the valley of death, and sustain me in the last struggle."

"Strange! You must n't leave me, Elsie. Your words drive away my horror. I will try to sleep," said Mrs. Billmer; and she soon fell into unquiet slumber.

Fanny was highly satisfied with the arrangement for the night made by Elsie, who, in the capacity of nurse, was to pass her first sleepless one. She was quite animated in feeling herself useful and necessary, and the thoughts of Thorsten kept her long wakeful. She thought of Aunt Lena, how many nights she had spent at sick-beds, and wondered if she never used to be sleepy. She watched the significant hour of twelve approach, and began to feel cold. She

could no longer conceal from herself the fact
that she was sleepy, when, suddenly, again Mrs.
Billmer awoke with a cry:

"I am in there again! Help! help!"

Elsie trembled, and her teeth chattered with
fright at the consciousness of inability to calm
either Mrs. Billmer or herself. However, she
made the effort.

"Dear friend," said she, "do n't you see
that there is no danger? You are resting in
your bed, and I am sitting with you. Would
you like some drops, or water?"

"No, thank you! it is gone now. I shall
try to sleep again," said Mrs. Billmer.

Again it was still. Elsie struggled against
sleep, and heard the bell proclaim the midnight
hour.

"Elsie," whispered Mrs. Billmer.

"Yes; here I am," responded Elsie.

"You are my friend, are you not? Will you
promise me, honestly and sincerely, to answer
the question I am going to ask you?"

"Yes," answered Elsie, without hesitation,
clasping her hands, as if for gathering strength.
She feared that her question would be of such
a nature as that her answer might cause a re-
newal of the scene upon the boat; and what
then should she do? Ought she not at once

to waken Fanny, and send her for the doctor?
for, come what may, she must speak the truth.

"Did you see me when I hung among the
bushes? there—you know?" asked Mrs. Billmer.

"Yes," replied Elsie.

"Tell me, then, sincerely—how did I appear?"

This question was so unexpected that Elsie
knew not how to answer it.

"I do n't understand you," said she.

"I wish to know if my appearance was ridiculous," said Mrs. Billmer.

"How could you think that a situation so
awful could to any one seem ridiculous?" said
Elsie.

"O, not at the time; but now, afterward,"
said Mrs. Billmer.   "Do n't you think that the
recollection of how I looked could make one
laugh—Judge Holt, for instance?"

"No, no; I can answer for him as for myself," asserted Elsie.

"You relieve my heart of a heavy load, if I
dare believe you," remarked Mrs. Billmer.

Elsie wondered if no heavier burden lay upon
this heart, no burden for sin; but she ventured
not to say any thing, and soon not only Mrs.
Billmer fell asleep, but her young nurse also.

Chapter XIX.

TAKING LEAVE.

OOR Elsie! how pale and tired you look!" said Axel, next morning, when he met his sister. "You must n't keep awake longer. Can not I do in your place?"

Elsie laughed at this proposal, and assured her brother that she was not tired—only a little low-spirited.

"Why?" asked Axel. "You know, I suppose, that Mrs. Billmer is in no danger?"

"Yes, I know the doctor said so. I am sorry about myself. Only think: I was sleeping so soundly in the morning when Fanny came in and Mrs. Billmer awoke, that they both laughed at me."

"And this wounded your dignity as a nurse? Consequently, not even you are exempt from human weakness," said Axel.

"O, how you talk!" said Elsie. "Who knows my weaknesses better than you do?"

Axel had a good mind to say that he considered her pretty free from fault in this case, but contented himself with placing a kiss of brotherly love and dignity upon her forehead, and admonishing her to be reasonable and not grieve for such a trifle.

"I have a matter of importance to speak with you about," he continued. "What do you think? Nollen has been to me, begging that I will act as his talisman with you. I was very much surprised at such a commission; but he told me he had been so unsuccessful in his attempts at soliciting your heart and hand that he despaired of success without assistance. Last night, he seemed to me so good-natured and kind in his readiness to help that I suppose I must have treated him in a more social, friendly manner than usual, and thus given him courage to open his heart."

"It was well that he turned to you," said Elsie, who the day previous had heard so many hints that she was not now surprised at the offer, but glad only to have the matter settled. "I suppose you gave him at once a decided refusal?"

"No, he did n't ask for me. He asked for you," said Axel.

"But you know that I never, never will have him for my husband."

"Why not?" asked Axel, with the indiscreet desire to pry out the secret sensations of his sister's heart.

"And you ask this—you, who think him so unendurable? I do not love him," said Elsie.

"Whom, then, do you love?" asked Axel.

"What a funny question!" said Elsie, blushing and confused. "I love father, aunt, and you."

"And Thorsten?" added Axel.

"Yes, Thorsten, too," said Elsie.

"Then Nollen has nothing to hope for?"

"No," replied Elsie; "but you must be very kind to him, and say that I am both sorry for and grateful to him."

"And that you bestow upon him your undying friendship?" added Axel.

"O, you mustn't make fun! He is so kind and upright; and last night his zeal in assisting was quite touching."

"O, do you begin with that tone? Perhaps you already repent your refusal?" said Axel.

"Of course not; but tell him it would make me really happy to hear soon that he had forgotten his sentiment for me, and that I wish him all good."

Elsie was now called for from the sick-room, and Axel promised to act with as much delicacy and courtesy as possible in giving Nollen her reply.

With sanguine anticipations, Elsie returned to her post as nurse. She thought that Mrs. Billmer, after some hours' sleep, would have so far recovered strength that she could converse with her about the grace of God, manifested to her in her great deliverance. It seemed natural to Elsie that the anguish by which, during the stillness of the night, Mrs. Billmer had been filled, should take, in the light of day, what she considered its real form—a deep and pungent grief for sin; and she thought what an unspeakable privilege it would be to whisper the true peace and comfort to her struggling spirit!

She entered the room cautiously, so as not to disturb the invalid, when the first sound that fell upon her listening ear was a heavy sigh.

"The doctor has been here," said Mrs. Billmer.

"Has he said any thing that troubles you?" asked Elsie.

"Yes, he has forbidden my receiving a single visit to-day. How long time will be!" said Mrs. Billmer.

"Do you think so? I think you rather ought to regard each moment as a precious gift," said Elsie, frightened at her own boldness.

"Heartless girl!" exclaimed Mrs. Billmer. "Will you remind me again of my escape from the chasm?"

Elsie and Mrs Billmer.

"Forgive me," said Elsie. "I was thinking of the great value of life, and how unmindful we all are of its brevity."

"No sermons, my dear!" said Mrs. Billmer. "My nerves are too weak for any thing of the kind. I am sufficiently besieged by my own thoughts. If you would read to me, perhaps I could listen."

"What do you wish to hear?" asked Elsie, a little discouraged at the failure of her efforts at conversation.

"I don't know. The novel I began yesterday isn't exactly suitable. I read only two chapters; but they told of six murders, and three or four other crimes; so that is somewhat too exciting for my poor nerves. Haven't you something interesting to offer?"

"Have you read 'Glimpses of the Human Heart,' by Lobstein?" asked Elsie.

"No, I don't know that author," said Mrs. Billmer. "If it isn't wild and sensational, like my novel—and one would imagine it to be so, from the title—you can try, if you please."

With pleasure, Elsie brought the book whose words she believed would prove so much more effectual than her own to lead Mrs. Billmer's thoughts where she desired; but the reading had hardly lasted ten minutes, when Mrs. Bill-

mer signified, by a motion, that it was to be
discontinued.

"Thank you; but this is a queer selection
for the occasion," said she. "I must acknowledge that I expected something of a quite different character. This is appropriate for Sunday
forenoon. Now I need something more enlivening; but your intentions were good."

"Another unsuccessful effort," thought Elsie,
with a sigh.

"Ask Fanny to come in," said Mrs. Billmer.
"I have just been thinking how I will dress to-
morrow. The doctor thinks I can go out into
the sitting-room then, and I shall receive calls.
It requires both taste and tact to arrange a
toilet suitable and becoming to a convalescent.
It should be at once tasty and unassuming."

The deliberations that now followed seemed
to Elsie so out of place that she withdrew to
seek advice from Mrs. Hervig. The old lady
listened to her in a manner that bespoke encouragement.

"I had hoped so much good would result
from this warning," said Elsie, sadly; and she
depicted to Mrs. Hervig the unchanged condition of Mrs. Billmer's mind, and how fruitless
were all her efforts to direct the thoughts of the
invalid.

"It would seem discouraging," said Mrs. Hervig; "but your youthful ardor has expected too much from an exterior occurrence. You hoped to see a sudden, great change, and you can not descry even a small one; but how can you or I know what the spirit of God may do in secret? Perhaps some seed has been sown that will one day germ to life—a spark fallen upon the hardened conscience that shall become a consuming fire. You must n't become weary in well-doing, even though it may seem to you that all your sympathy is overlooked and despised."

"No," said Elsie, "I trust that my interest is warm and lively; but it is such a trial to me to seek in vain for words that can touch her heart."

"Words can reach the heart; but they can also be forgotten," said Mrs. Hervig. "Leave in her memory the picture of a cheerful, gentle, patient Christian, and you have given her more than words; and then, firstly and lastly, pray— pray for her and for yourself!"

While Mrs. Hervig was speaking, Thorsten had entered, and, with manifest emotion, was contemplating Elsie, who was listening so attentively to the words of her aged friend as not to have noticed when the door was opened.

"My time is so brief," said Thorsten, "pardon what may seem my selfishness, if I interrupt conversation."

"Your time so brief? Do you think, dear Judge, to leave us before the appointed time?" asked Mrs. Hervig.

"Yes, I have just received a letter that necessitates my departure," answered Thorsten. "I had intended to remain some days longer; but, as it is, I must leave Marstrand at noon. I am very glad to meet you here," said he to Elsie. "I feared that you would be so occupied with Mrs. Billmer as to render it difficult for me to find an opportunity for bidding you good-bye."

Elsie tried to answer, but failed. The treacherous tears poured forth again and again. She was ashamed of her childishness. Why could she not, in a calm, friendly manner, tell him she was sorry, very sorry, that he must leave them so soon? She did not know. Thorsten spoke with Mrs. Hervig about his journey, so that Elsie had time for quieting her emotions.

"When are you coming to Stockholm?" she asked, as Thorsten's look again rested upon her.

"Next Fall."

"Not before? That is more than a year," said Elsie.

"Yes, it is a long time,".he replied; "but you must n't forget me."

He tried to speak in a jovial manner; but his voice betrayed an emotion that gave to his words a deep and earnest signification. Elsie extended him her hand, saying, as she did so:

"Good-bye, Thorsten."

"Not yet," he replied, and kept her back. "You must n't leave us so soon."

"Yes, I must," she replied. "Mrs. Billmer is waiting for me, and—"

The tears could no longer be repressed.

"You must take an adieu to Mrs. Billmer for me," said Thorsten. "Tell her I am sorry I can not see her to speak it myself, and that I hope she will soon be recovered;" and, quickly carrying her hand to his lips, he whispered, "God bless you!"

Elsie had gone. Thorsten stood gazing after her; then, suddenly turning to Mrs. Hervig, he said:

"Am I a hero or a coward to let her go alone?"

Mrs. Hervig smiled at the unexpected question, and said:

"Do not demand judgment without investigation, my dear jurist."

"I forbear to see her alone, and feel myself

heroic; but is it not cowardly to do so for fear of losing one's self-control?"

"'Better fly than fight poorly,' says the proverb; and I can not deny, my dear Judge, that, if you hold to your resolution to withhold from her the real character of your regard for her, it were high time to take flight," said Mrs. Hervig, laughing.

"Yes, that's true; but I dislike to leave her with Mrs. Billmer. My hope is in you, Mrs. Hervig. Take good care of her."

"It would be sad if your hope had no better stay than in me," replied Mrs. Hervig; "but rest assured it will be my highest pleasure to be of any service to Elsie. Her society is to me like the presence of a mild Spring day."

Chapter XX.

HOMEWARD BOUND.

AFTER the departure of Thorsten, Elsie began to realize that Mrs. Billmer was not altogether mistaken in her opinion of the surroundings of Marstrand. She longed for home.

Mrs. Billmer's nervous system soon regained the elasticity it had lost for a few days; and no rose, swayed by the wind, more easily shakes off the trembling dew-drop than did her soul seem to rid itself of every serious thought concerning her great deliverance.

All Elsie's hopes for a truer sympathy between them disappeared entirely. Perhaps, as Mrs. Hervig had suggested, a spark had fallen upon the heart of Mrs. Billmer that some day became a refining fire. We do not know.

In her character as "Mercy," Mrs. Billmer received much praise for the true conception and excellent execution she displayed; but, whether all the pleasures of this occasion would counterbalance the modest gratitude which Elsie received from the bright-eyed little girl for whom she assisted Mrs. Hervig in procuring clothes, we leave it to the reader to decide, hoping he has himself experienced what joy there is in bringing sunshine to the heart of a little child already familiar with want and self-denial.

Axel had become tired of his dreamings upon the sea. Now his thoughts were occupied only with the journey abroad, to which he hoped his father would consent.

The day of departure came. When Elsie had bidden good-bye to her aged friend, Mrs. Hervig, and felt herself blush at the happy assurance with which she spoke of a future meeting, she found Mrs. Billmer waiting for the steamer, weeping, and embracing all her friends, who, at the moment of adieu, were so dear.

"Well, Elsie, are you here at last?" she cried. "I have been waiting for you half an hour, in mortal anguish."

"But the steamer isn't here yet; why have you been so anxious?" asked Elsie.

"O, I was afraid you would be too late to take a last farewell of all these dear friends of ours who have gathered here to see us depart," said she; adding, in a whisper, "You certainly can speak a friendly word to Nollen, who stands there, waiting with a bouquet for you, and looking so unhappy."

"Yes; I would like to show him my friendly feeling toward him," said Elsie, touched at the sadness of his countenance.

"Good-bye, Lieutenant Nollen," said she; "thanks for all your kindness. Forgive me if, contrary to my intention, I have wounded—"

"The steamer! Dearest Elsie! Good-bye!"

These words were showered by some young ladies, who ran up and interrupted Elsie's little farewell speech with an attack of kisses and embraces so violent that Elsie became quite dizzy; and with a kind of relief she heard the signal for starting, and saw the boat move from the landing, where the fluttering handkerchiefs kept up their adieus.

We have now left Marstrand, and taken leave of Mrs. Billmer, whose graceful form now glides away, no more to appear in our story.

Should some compassionate heart interest itself for Nollen, we can say that two months had not elapsed, after the events here narrated, when hundreds of little white messengers were sent out to the world to announce an engagement between "Adalbert Nollen and Euphrasia

Filibom," a solid beauty, who, to be sure, had outlived her earliest bloom, but, what was better, her rich, parsimonious papa also. Some, given to thinking evil, will of course predict that the beautiful Euphrasia will hold the purse-strings herself, and that, with the money, she has inherited also her father's ear for the clink-ing of gold, wherefore the future of our friend Nollen may not be wholly exempt from thorns.

Chapter XXI.

"ALL IS WELL THAT ENDS WELL."

GAIN it was Autumn, as when we made our first visit to the Stark family. But it is not, as at the time of our first visit, a heavy, dark, rainy day. The atmosphere is clear and bright, and, although the sun has already disappeared, the western glow sheds an enlivening roseate hue over land and water, and the tumultuous city.

However, in the offices of wholesale dealer Stark no poetic half-days gain rule. The lamps are lighted, and busy pens go flying over the paper.

In the inner room, the private office of merchant Stark himself, the silence is unbroken by even the faint sound of a pen. Absorbed in thought, he leans his head upon his hand. Is it the anniversary of his marriage, or of his bereavement, that calls forth this sad, weary expression? Neither. For a long time he has looked upon the past without bitterness. The thought of his departed wife was one full of blessed hope. He felt that they were united in the same faith, and that each passing year brought him nearer the blessedness to which she had attained.

He feels lonely and tired. His ability for work begins to give out; and there is no one at his side to whom, with full confidence, he can resign a part of the care of his business. To be sure, his efforts have been blessed, and he trusts he can leave to each of his children an independent fortune; but how uncertain was this hope, should he in these unquiet times be obliged to leave in part the management of his extensive business into stranger, and perhaps dishonest, hands! Deceit and fraud belong to the order of the day, and have thrown even into the honest soul of Mr. Stark a shade of suspicion.

This thought troubles him; but there is another one that troubles yet more his paternal heart—the thought of his dear only son, who now, during a whole year, has been a wanderer in foreign lands, seeking, without being able to find, the peace he has lost. During the first months of his absence, his letters home were frequent, and breathed a hope that had awakened a joyful echo there; but then they became less frequent and briefer, and, although they evidently evaded giving all that pertained to his inner life, they wore the stamp of discouragement and disappointed anticipations. Now, week after week had passed without bringing even one of these short letters, and the anxiety concerning him grew daily. Perhaps he lay ill, or even dying, among strangers.

It was nothing strange that, while the merchant's thoughts were thus occupied, he was unmindful of the presence of a stranger who had passed quickly through the outer rooms, and, without asking permission, had come directly into his private office.

"Forgive me, if I disturb you," said a well-intonated voice.

"Thorsten!" cried the merchant, in surprise, drawing his hand across his forehead, as if to pass off from his mind the heavy clouds that had overcast it, and, whether it was this motion of his hand that removed the clouds, or whether they were dispersed by the irresistible smile that met his eye, sure it is that he seemed very cheerful as he added: "Welcome, sincerely welcome, my dear boy! When did you come?"

"Just now."

"Then you have n't seen Aunt Lena and Elsie?"

"No; I wished first to see you, my friend and benefactor, to ask a question that concerns my future happiness."

"O, you are thinking of marriage, I judge, from your serious manner," said the merchant, and smiled encouragingly.

"You understand me, then, already?"

"Yes, yes; but you need a little assistance to start with. Your income is good; but it seems to me quite natural that you have been unable to lay aside any capital. It will be a pleasure to me to be at your service."

"Do n't misunderstand me," exclaimed Thorsten. "With pride and pleasure I can say that my own endeavors have provided a home for my future wife. I can not offer wealth and luxury; but I can offer a home without debt, and a heart with love as warm and sincere as was ever offered to woman."

The merchant observed with pleasure the open, manly earnestness of the speaker, while at the same time he fingered the key of his safe, quite puzzled at what could be the purport of Thorsten's question.

"Since you need no pecuniary help, what can I do for you?" he asked.

"Give me Elsie."

"Impossible!" exclaimed the merchant, start-ing from his chair as if struck with consterna-tion, which was accompanied by such vehemence of gesture as, to a spectator less interested than Thorsten, might have seemed ludicrous, but upon him produced a very painful impression. Becoming pale, he asked:

"How? Am I too late?"

"Too late?" repeated the merchant. "What do you mean? Too early, much too early!" and he began nervously pacing the floor.

The warm color returned to Thorsten's cheeks as he asked:

"Is Elsie's youthfulness the only objection?"

"Yes. As if that were not a sufficient one!" exclaimed the merchant.

"But she is in her twentieth year, and is no longer a child, although the innocent simplicity of her manners gives her a much younger ap-pearance than have others of her age. It is more than a year since I saw her last; but is she not the same as then?"

"Yes; yet—no, not exactly," said Mr. Stark. "She hasn't been quite herself since her trip to Marstrand. She is less buoyant than before. She has sometimes an expression in her eye that reminds me of her poor mother, when she used to relapse into reverie; but, thank God! her mother's heavy sigh I have not heard from my Elsie. She is happy and healthful; finds pleasure in her work, and interest in helping and causing happiness wherever she can."

"You acknowledge thus that she is more developed, less a child and more a woman, than when I saw her last," said Thorsten; "and it was then only through much struggle and effort that I forbore telling her how dear she was to me. But it seemed to me then too early. She met me with such loving confidence, such joy at seeing a friend of her childhood, that, had I then propounded the question that was in my heart, she would certainly have answered 'yes,' without thoroughly understanding her own heart. But I was unwilling as a thief to win her; so I resolved to keep silent and wait, and not see her again until she had completed her nineteenth year."

"Thank you!" said the merchant; "you acted honorably. And, as far as my consent goes, I wish you to understand that no man could be more acceptable to me as a son-in-law than you; but Elsie's happiness is involved, and sooner ask my life than that by a single word I should attempt to influence her in her choice."

"I neither ask nor wish this, only the right to speak with Elsie myself," said Thorsten.

"Yes; but when you speak, will she not, from esteem to you and confidence in you, and to please me, answer yes?"

"Can love, then, have a better and more solid foundation than esteem and confidence?" asked Thorsten.

"Well, well, this sounds well enough; but, you see, I know how it really is to have a wife who said yes from a sense of esteem and filial duty. God save you both from such a misfortune!"

"Forgive me for touching upon a subject so tender," said Thorsten; "but I think that the circumstances surrounding Elsie can not be compared with those in which her mother was placed. Were you not a stranger to her, and her education more calculated for calling forth a sickly sentimentality than an open look at the true value of life?"

"Yes; it was so," replied the merchant.

"It may seem strange that I should judge circumstances that I never saw; but what little has fallen upon my ear concerning your marriage, taken in connection with my observation of similar cases, has produced upon me this conviction."

The merchant stood meditating, and Thorsten continued:

"Elsie has enjoyed the blessings of a Christian home. Whatever her destiny may be, she will never be the victim to an overwrought fancy or a relaxing indolence. She knows that she is a woman and a Christian, and life is to her no misty, dreamy picture. Her aim is high. She is natural and true, and will not deceive either us or herself. How could she hide a thought in her pure soul? Leave, then, the decision to her. Does she love me? O, let me hear it from her lips! Has she only friendship to give me? I promise by no word or look to influence her sympathies. Be yourself present at our first meeting as witness, and judge. Perhaps I am myself unfit to judge impartially of the answer I shall receive."

"Thank you! God bless you! Come, let us go immediately home," said the merchant.

Thorsten was not slow to obey the summons; and soon after we see both gentlemen entering the pleasantly lighted sitting-room, where Miss Lena and Elsie are busy at their sewing, forming a picture of domestic happiness and quiet. A magnificent bouquet of Autumn flowers, and a basket of delicious fruit, contributed with their fresh colors to the enlivenment of the scene;

while some new books and the open piano witnessed that the needle was sometimes laid aside for other occupation.

Elsie arose to meet her father; and when she saw Thorsten, joy beamed from her eyes, and her cheeks glowed; but suddenly became again pale, and she stood trembling.

"Do I frighten you, Elsie?" said Thorsten, seizing both her hands.

"No, no; I am so glad!" she answered.

"You are so surprised?" asked Thorsten.

"No; I have been looking for you," said Elsie, artlessly. "You promised to come in the Fall; and I called it Fall early this year," she added, endeavoring with a jest to hide her emotion and the violent throbbing of her heart.

"Elsie, dare I hope that the question I have come to ask you is also not unexpected?"

Her head drooped modestly, and she saw not the warm look that rested upon her; but did she not feel it? Did it not shed light and warmth through her whole being? Thorsten drew her to him, and whispered:

"Elsie, will you become my wife?"

What would she answer? The father stood waiting, in breathless suspense, to hear; but, as far as words are concerned, he might have remained in utter uncertainty, for no sound from

Elsie reached his ear. And yet she must have replied. What else meant this long embrace; this exclamation of transport, "Thank you, my precious one!" these kisses, those beaming, tearful glances?

The merchant had ample time for making these reflections, and drying his spectacles, which had a peculiar tendency to become dim.

Finally, the young people seemed to remember that they were not the only creatures in the universe, and Elsie, hastening to her father, threw herself into his arms.

"Father, dear father," said she, "I am so happy!"

The merchant made a feeble effort to raise a doubt as to the character of her feelings.

"How can you know that you love him?" he asked.

"Father," said she, "how do you know it is Spring, when all nature exults in the newly awakened life of a precious May-day? That is the way it seems in my heart, only a thousand times happier and brighter than any earthly Spring day can be."

"But," said the father, "if I should see Spring develop within the space of five minutes, I should be very much inclined to regard it as an illusion of my senses."

"O father," said Elsie, "do n't think that I have n't loved Thorsten before now;" and, as she spoke, her eye met Thorsten's, and she hid her blushes in her father's bosom.

"Child," said the father, stroking her light hair, "may God's blessing rest upon you, and his hand guide you along the way that now appears to you so bright, but which to you even will not be without cares and troubles! Bear them mutually, and as Christians. You have been the sunshine of my life, Elsie; be the same to your husband also. Take her, Thorsten—or, rather, keep her; for she is already yours."

The reader has perhaps, like the three actors in this scene, forgotten the presence of a fourth, whose heart was throbbing with the warmest sympathy. Lena had for a long time suspected Elsie's secret; but she was restrained from drawing out her confidence by the same womanly delicacy that caused Elsie to withhold it.

Lena was therefore quite prepared for what would take place when Thorsten should come, although she had not expected it so immediately upon his arrival. She was happy in seeing the happiness of her pet, and that she could believe in its endurance; for Thorsten had always stood high in Aunt Lena's regard. But, when the year before he had spent a few days with the old people before going to Marstrand, her friendship for him had taken yet deeper root. He had openly and earnestly spoken of his hope, and she had found in him a rich development of grace and wisdom. Although they did not agree in all respects upon certain Scriptural points, their disputes were without contest, and furnished refreshing exercise for thought and faith. They both stood upon one platform.

Yes, Lena rejoiced; and yet, should we analyze the tear that is falling from her eye, would we find joy to be its only ingredient? We believe there is in it, too, a trifle of sadness at the memory of a joyless youth.

Shall we smile in contempt at the old lady's half-unconscious perception of never having been young?

No; let the poor tear fall unnoticed. It is already away, and Aunt Lena too is participating in congratulations and embraces.

We will wait now until all are quietly seated for the evening. Aunt Lena's knitting is going at full speed; but Elsie's work rests, and yet the time does not drag, thanks to her neighbor.

The merchant is paring an apple, and trying to familiarize himself with new circumstances, but seems restless and confused. Now and then he casts a smiling look upon the betrothed ones, sometimes a sad one into the past, and at the next moment he anxiously consults the clock.

"The mail ought to be in now," he remarked. "It must bring a letter from Axel."

"O, how selfish I am!" exclaimed Elsie. "To-night I have n't had a thought about Axel. Dear Axel! When shall we see him again?"

"Where is he?" asked Thorsten.

"We know not," replied Mr. Stark. "His last letter was from Geneva; but that came more than two months ago, and we have had no reply to the many letters we have written him since then; so we are very anxious."

While her father was speaking, Elsie had hastened to meet a servant bringing the mail.

"Here it is!" she exclaimed joyfully, and held up a letter. "This is Axel's handwriting and the Geneva stamp; so he has received all we have sent, and yet has been so long silent."

The merchant opened the letter and began reading; but his voice soon failed him, while tears of the purest joy dimmed his eyes; and he passed it to Thorsten, who proceeded as follows:

"DEAR ONES AT HOME:

"How much cause I have given you for dissatisfaction by the irregularity of my correspondence during the year in which I have been a rover abroad; yet I am glad that it has been irregular; for so my last long interval of silence has given you less anxiety than you would otherwise have experienced. I have been ill—seriously so, I believe; but rejoice with me! Life has been victorious—not physical life only, but, too, that of the spirit. I am now again well; and the first use I make of my strength is to communicate to you, in a manner as clear and definite as possible, my experiences during this time; but remember that I am a convalescent, both in body and spirit. My heart is so full of joy and praise that I can not calmly and clearly develop my thoughts.

"My last was written you from Geneva, where I threw my whole soul into the theological controversies, carried on by men of talent and genius. I belonged to no party, but sought for the real views of each controversialist. My courage was quickened. I thought that here, if anywhere, I must find the truth. I heard wit, eloquence, and learning—all that could enlighten and disperse the darkness of my soul, I thought; and I believed myself at the end of my search. I worked and worked, and did not perceive how I was becoming deeply engaged in systems and dogmas, without coming any nearer to Christ.

Theology became to me as dangerous as philosophy had been. The truth was by truth obscured
from my vision. My courage again failed. I became hopeless and weary. An oppressive head-
ache frequently interrupted my researches. There
were moments in which I feared for my reason.

"One evening, when, as usual, I was sitting
deeply engaged in study, I was visited by a
young Switzer, a Mr. Bernard, whose acquaintance I had formed at some theological lecture.
Bernard is a cheerful, good-hearted man, who
became interested in me, so he says, because
we are so utterly unlike. When, for a while,
he had sat contemplating me, his look became
uncommonly serious; then he said:

. "'I have come to extend you an invitation
which you must accept. A few of us have resolved to make an excursion among the mountains, to get a little rest from study. To us, rest
is more a pleasure than a necessity; but to you
it is a duty to tear away from your overwork.'

"I felt that he was right, and longed to get
out amid nature. Preparations were soon made,
and we started. There were six of us. Subject
for conversation was not wanting. My companions were educated, intellectual men, and soon
discussion took the form of lively dispute; for
sentiments the most various were represented—

belief and disbelief, Christ and Belial. I wished
to be a defender of the faith, but to this end
felt weak before its antagonists. I lacked both
the sword of the Spirit and the shield of faith.

"On the third day of our wandering, we
came to a beautiful valley. However, it did
not at first appear to us in its beauty; for, as
we were entering it, we were surprised by a violent shower, which made us think more of seeking protection than admiring the meadow. Wet
through, we reached a rustic dwelling, where we
were hospitably received by a friendly matron.
My comrades hung their wet clothes before the
great fire-place, and supplied their lack, as far
as possible, from the scanty furnishing of their
valises.

"My head burned, while I shook with cold
chills. The merriment of the rest seemed to me
noisy and disagreeable. Slowly, and with effort,
too, I got off my wet clothes, and wrapped myself in a woolen blanket, which our kind hostess
had brought in, among other things, to serve as
substitute for clothing. The care of the matron
seemed in particular for me. She gave me a
motherly look, and placed me in a chair by the
fire. I sat down, surprised at the unpleasant
stiffness I felt in all my joints. I was sleepy,
and yet could not sleep. With half-shut eyes, I

leaned my head against the high back of my chair, and saw how the gayety of my friends disappeared, and that a whispered conversation arose between them and the hostess, while the looks of all were fixed upon me. I could not understand what they were saying, and only felt a dull indifference to myself and the whole world.

"How long I remained sitting thus, I know not. After a while, I could discern no definite object. All became a confused mass, from which glared at me a fearful multitude of eyes. The only other recollection I have of this day is of being placed in bed by Bernard and Katherine, my hostess. For a moment, it seemed good to stretch my aching limbs; but my fatigue was so great that I felt as if fixed to the bed. Afterward, I heard how Bernard, with brotherly tenderness, made arrangements for me, procured me a physician, sent me clothes from Geneva, and, as he could not himself remain to nurse me, recommended me to the care of Katherine and her husband, who proved themselves worthy of confidence.

"The doctor pronounced my disease typhoid fever, probably at first induced by over-exertion, and afterward developed by a cold, and only ordered that I should be kept perfectly quiet, and frequently given a cooling drink. What

wonderful grace was there in the arrangement
that led me here to find healing for both body
and spirit! Far away from the noisy world, I
was lying in a quiet home, a place of refuge,
which the Lord himself had opened to me.
Katherine and Joseph (for that is the name of
her husband) are real Christians. Their position
in life is humble but independent. They have
nursed me as if I were a dear son, and not a
stranger. God bless them!

"Two weeks passed without any apparent
change. I lay in stupor during the day-time,
while at night the fever raged more violently,
and I talked at random. I have only a vague
recollection of a nameless anguish, and a constantly vain effort to escape from theological and
philosophical disputes. Thus, on the fifteenth
night also, I lay suffering great pain. What I
said, I know not; but what I can never forget is
the earnest, furrowed countenance that bent over
me, as a calm, clear voice said:

"'This is a faithful saying, and worthy of
all acceptation, that Christ Jesus came into the
world to save sinners.'

"Words can not describe my feelings. Peace
filled my soul. 'A faithful saying!' What more
did I need? I was saved! A feeling of wonder without fear went through me, whether this

peace belonged to life, or I was standing upon the border of eternity, with the quiet of death surrounding me. A feeble 'Amen!' was the only response I could make; yet I felt as if my voice were mingling in the chorus of angels, and rising upward to the throne of the holy triune God!

"For the first time since my illness began, I fell into a refreshing sleep, which lasted during twelve hours, when I woke to full consciousness. Of course, my body was prostrated by weakness and disease; but my spirit was strong and free. The light that arose in my soul at Joseph's cital of the 'faithful saying' was no illusion. I believe I know now what the new birth is. When Thorsten comes to you, as I think he soon will, tell him that a blessed experience has forever silenced in me the Nicodemus question.

"Physical strength now returned quickly. The physician charged me for a time to refrain from all mental work; but thought is no longer fatiguing to me. On the contrary, I find repose in it; but I do not as yet read. It is refreshing to me to listen while Katherine and Joseph read aloud from the Bible. Their simple, earnest faith has been more useful to me than the discourses of learned divines. It has been an immediate conducting to the well itself.

"Has all my research, then, been to no use—
all my former reading and hearing only a dis-
tancing from God? I have asked myself these
questions, and each time the answer has been a
cheerful, plainer 'No.' I believe that I have
gathered many a seed that shall become a fruit-
ful plant. Once they lay enveloped in the darkness of my spirit, knowledge without life; now
the sun of grace has dispelled the darkness, and
its warming rays shall awaken in them life and
growth. I look back with painful surprise upon
my unbelief. How simple does the truth appear
when one has found it! How unlike all human
work! Did I say that I had found the truth?
No. It was not so. I am found. See here
the solution of life's enigma—the joy that fills
my soul with light, life, and strength.

"To-day, when I opened my window, a dense
fog overspread the landscape. I could see nothing; and yet I knew that the sun was shining,
and that the valley lay outspread before me, as
beautiful as ever; and I felt the beauty of the
hymn:

'Dispel, Lord, the darkness of doubt;
Let me light from thy countenance see.'

Yes, a mist, a darkness had separated me from
God; and all these doubts, this perplexity and
anguish, are dispelled by the sun of grace, and

the assurance of God's love revealed in Jesus Christ. In my blindness, I thought that human reason had demolished the foundations. The mist rolled away, and I saw that nothing had lost aught of its harmonious beauty. The foundations are laid in eternity, and shall endure forever. What though I can not comprehend all? The sun is shining also beyond the range of my weak vision. I know that I have much to learn, and that life calls me to a ceaseless activity.

"A life of study is unsuited to me; its temptations I have tried. I long to begin a life of practical usefulness. You, father, have given me regard for real work. You have never by a word sought to influence my choice of vocation. I feel a deep gratitude for your kindness; and my wish is to take my place at your side, supported by your experience, and supporting your old age. Work will thus become light to us both, will it not? And the acquirement of money shall not be our object, but the use of it in the service of our Master.

"In a few days I shall leave this place, which to me will be so memorable. Like Jacob, I would wish to raise a stone, with the inscription, 'This is none other but the house of God, and this is the gate of heaven;' for, like him, I have seen heaven open, and the angels of God ascending and descending.

"After a short visit in Geneva, I shall hasten northward to the dear old home, where I am hoping to feel quite at home, now that, with my loved ones there, I can unite in the song of redemption.

"God's peace rest upon you! as it rests now upon   Your happy   AXEL.

"P. S.—Thanks, Aunt Lena, for all the Scripture texts you taught me when I was a child. They came up in memory one after another, and were very refreshing to me, when I could neither hear nor read."

"Blessed be the name of the Lord from this time forth and for ever more!" exclaimed Aunt Lena.

The merchant bowed his head upon his folded hands in silent thanksgiving, while the younger ones began a song of praise.

Axel's decision to engage in his father's business gave great satisfaction. The elder ones would not be alone when Elsie should leave them, and Thorsten could so much the more easily make known his arrangements for the future, and his wish to take Elsie home as his wife in the Spring.

His old friend, Judge Dangel, had offered him, in case he should marry, the second story of his spacious residence, which was now mostly unoccupied. A few repairs and alterations would render the rooms very commodious for their use, and paper and pencils appeared for the clearer representation of locality and alterations. Suggestions were made, expenses calculated, and those numerous little matters talked over which usually occupy considerable attention during the period of betrothal, and are so pleasant to the parties interested.

At night, when Lena retired, she could not help saying, as she looked into Elsie's beaming eyes:

"Child, you appear so happy that I feel fear for you. Do not let your earthly joy obscure your joy in God."

"O, no, no!" exclaimed Elsie. "My happiness lifts me on strong wings above earth. I know that life at Thorsten's side will be a journey with him upward, in the same faith, toward the same goal."

THE END.

www.ingramcontent.com/pod-product-compliance
Lightning Source LLC
Chambersburg PA
CBHW031429020726
47499CB00005B/1662